DOG GONE

DOG GONE

CYNTHIA CHAPMAN WILLIS

SCHOLASTIC INC.
New York   Toronto   London   Auckland
Sydney   Mexico City   New Delhi   Hong Kong

ISBN 978-0-545-29724-0

12 11 10 9 8 7 6 5 4 3 2 1   10 11 12 13 14 15/0

Printed in the U.S.A.   40

First Scholastic printing, September 2010

*In memory of my father,
Laighton D. Chapman,
and the dog we loved*

CHAPTER 1

GOOD DOG

"Y our dog stinks worse than roadkill, Dill," Cub says, wrinkling his nose and puckering his face in a look that screams disgust. His arms strain under the old tin tub that's holding Mom's flowery-scented shampoo, a few old towels, Dead End's dog brush, a plastic cup for rinsing, and a rawhide bone big enough to choke an elephant.

"Which is exactly why he's getting a bath with the most sweet-smelling shampoo I could dig up." Even the usual barn smells of hay, oats, and dusty chickens are being overpowered by the sour stench rising off the wet, greenish-brown smudges that mat the blond fur of Dead End's muzzle, shoulders, and sides. How a pooch could stink himself up so bad is beyond my twelve-year-old imagination.

"Sweet-smelling shampoo," Cub mutters under his breath. "Just like a girl."

Dead End pulls toward the door, determined to break free of his leash, even if that means snapping my wrist in two like some dried twig. I manage to get the plastic bag out from the pocket of my shirt. And sure enough, the second I toss Dead End the last of the cranberry-raisin cookies that I'd baked, he forgets about freedom and snatches the thing without losing a crumb. These cookies are his favorite treat. Still, I can't help but be impressed by his catch.

I let the plastic bag fall from my fingers. As Dead End starts snuffling it, looking for more cookies, I pull the barn door as closed as it will go. But there's still a gap—a problem as big as Virginia itself because this dog of mine has to be kept inside this building.

CLANG! Cub drops the aluminum tub on the floor, by the hay bales. The towels go flying. The bone bounces out and thuds, barely misses his big toe.

"If G.D. sees Dead End this filthy, he'll know he's been running again," I say, watching the silly pooch get his snout stuck in the plastic bag. "He could tell Lyon." My dad. "And that man is in no mood for a misbehaving dog."

"You haven't said anything about that dog takin' off again to your granddad or your dad?" Cub shakes his head, disapproving.

This is pure Cub, always about truth and playing by the rules. A kid with a conscience a mile long, one reason why he's been my friend since the beginning of first grade, when we bonded over trying to find a way to put a baby bird back into its nest. That connection became glue when we spent most of the next summer and every school break since together, making our own fun because we live miles away from all our other school friends. And our bond has turned to cement in the last year, because Cub has been here without me asking him to be. He's stayed close during everything that's happened. And he's here still.

"Dill, keepin' that dog's runnin' a secret is bad," he tells me, like I don't know this. "What about the promise you made to your dad?"

"Dead End has only run off a few times in the last three months." *Since Mom left,* I don't add. "Besides, if Lyon finds out, he'll take the dog to a shelter."

Dead End sneezes hard, the way he does whenever I have a leash on him. The plastic bag goes flying.

It is no secret that Lyon came within a hair of getting rid of Dead End right after G.D., my granddad, brought the pooch to us four years ago. The dog only ran away twice and returned on his own both times, but he'd been caught chasing a few chickens and got into some garbage. Nothing major, but Lyon wouldn't have it: *We can't keep a dog that takes off,* he announced in his flat-out, no-nonsense tone, slamming down his decision like an ax blade. *Keeping a dog that pesters others is irresponsible.*

No surprise the dog runs, G.D. had said. *He's been a stray, probably for some time.* But G.D. also believed the dog was ready to settle down, needed to. So I made a deal with Lyon, promised him that if he gave Dead End one more chance at being good, I'd solemnly swear to keep an eye on him and report the first sign of any more bad behavior.

"Doesn't your dad know what shelters do?" Cub makes a violent slashing motion with his hand at his throat.

I shrug as Dead End starts pulling again, yanking at my wrist. Mom had known. Right after Lyon and I made our deal, she'd taken the pooch to Sarah Doyle's obedience classes, transforming him into a good dog that didn't run off. Everyone but Mom saw this as a true miracle, but her sixth sense about animals had told her that he'd become a devoted pet. And he had. Devoted to her, mostly.

That's why, it seems to me, he's started running again: because she's gone. Our once warm and full home is cold and hollow, with sadness collecting like dust. Not even a day after she'd left us, the pooch started pacing and whining, pawing at the door of the master bedroom. If someone were to ask me, which no one would because I've made it as clear as crystal that I won't talk about her, I'd say Dead End is searching for Mom.

I'd take off, too, even leave Virginia itself, if I could get up the guts to cut away from Lyon and G.D., I've whispered in the dog's ear more than once.

"It doesn't matter what Lyon knows," I answer Cub. "He'll get rid of Dead End the way he's been getting rid of everything that reminds him of what was." By *what was*, I mean life with Mom in it. Lyon has, despite all my protests, placed most of her loved and pampered pets in new homes. Her rabbits (Romeo, Juliet, and their five thousand babies), her goat (Seymour—blind in one eye), and the barn cats (Double and Trouble, adopted from an animal shelter). But Dead End got to stick around. Probably because the dog was Mom's favorite. But that doesn't mean Lyon will put up with any nonsense.

As Dead End keeps yanking at the leash and sneezing, I breathe in the background mustiness of the chickens, Annie and Dan, the only tenants left in this barn. And only because Lyon can't catch them.

Cub sighs, swipes at sweat beading on his forehead and hay clinging to his brown hair, which sticks up from his head like the bristles of a toothbrush (his mom buzzes the heads of her five boys the first day of each summer). Then he moves to the stacked hay bales against the back wall, focusing on a fly bouncing against the screen of a window propped open with a stick at the top of the hay. "I swear that dog hates leashes worse than fleas. Is allergic to them. Better let him loose before he takes your arm off, Dill." Cub hikes up his sagging shorts and begins climbing the bales like a mountain goat.

"You need to rig the barn door to shut first," I tell him. Given wire or twine, Cub can attach, bind, or mend anything. Lyon calls this a gift. I call it convenient.

Cub scoops the fly into his fist, climbs down the hay bales, and scuffs across the floor, pausing only to pick up the rawhide bone with his free hand. At the doorway, he uncurls his fist, setting the fly free.

Curious as a cat and always looking for something to eat, Dead End near strangles himself trying to get to Cub and sniff his fly hand. Cub bunches up his face, yanks the T-shirt collar over his nose, and hands the pooch the bone. "Here, Stinky."

Dead End swings his tail in big O's that say *Thanks!* and show he's happier than a pig in mud.

"I'll need bailing twine to hold this door closed," Cub says, eyeing the latch.

"There's a pile of it by the garden," I tell him.

As he steps outside, I drop to a squat and begin massaging Dead End's neck where the green-brown stains aren't thick and nasty. "I don't care what you've rolled in," I tell him, but I breathe through my mouth, not my nose. And I clutch the leash as if it's a hundred-dollar bill because I don't need the dog taking off again.

With two miles of tongue hanging out one side of his mouth, the yellow Labrador-husky mix with the curled tail, pointed ears, and big brown eyes fringed in golden eyelashes gazes up at me as if to say *Don't worry about me. I'm a good dog!*

A good dog that G.D. came upon behind a Dumpster at the end of a dead-end street somewhere in New Jersey. *Named the dog after the road I found him on,* G.D. had told me. *Needed to call him something.* Dead End *came out as less of a mouthful than Southwest General George Washington Highway.*

To me, the dog's odd name was a clear-sky sign that he belonged with us. Mom and Lyon named me Dylan after their favorite singer—before they knew that my singing voice made animals howl and small children cry. It didn't even matter to them that I'd been born a girl—I still got a man's last name. Cub, the youngest of the six Bayer boys, had been given his nickname, which replaced *Kenneth,* the minute he'd been born. Lyon hardly ever goes by *Dad,* and G.D. has never been *Granddad.* Even Mom's name, *Summer,* wasn't ordinary. But it fit her. Like summertime, she'd been warm, easy, and carefree.

And like every summertime I'd known, she didn't last long enough.

Never meant for the name Dead End *to stick,* G.D. had said. *Never thought the dog would stick. He was thin and scrappy, with no collar or tags. Weeks passed, but the dog kept hanging around. We got used to each other and the name* Dead End.

As Cub steps back into the barn with loops of bailing twine, he starts knotting and tying. "Keepin' that dog's runnin' secret from your dad is wrong, Dill. You made him a promise, gave him your word. That's sacred."

Before I can ask how he, an animal-loving veterinarian wannabe, could even think about turning Dead End in and risk losing him, the dog's ears pop up at full attention.

Jingling! My heart sinks at that sound of the engagement and wedding rings that G.D. wears near his heart, on a chain under his T-shirts. I jump up, grab hold of Dead End's collar, and pull him toward a stall. Stubborn as a two-ton mule, he leans away from me. "Cub . . ." My whisper comes out a strained gasp. "Help me hide this dog."

Cub drops the twine, grabs hold of Dead End's collar, and starts pulling the pooch as I attack the rusted latch of the stall door, trying to slide it back.

The jingling gets louder. "This stinking piece of scrap metal won't budge!" And one slip means I'll have more splinters than a pincushion has needles.

Cub grunts. "This dog should be named *Dead Weight*."

"Dill? Dylan MacGregor?" G.D.'s wavering voice sends my thudding heart into overdrive. "You in the barn, girl?"

Dead End whines. My heart thumps harder: *Don't get caught! Don't get caught! Don't get caught!* I lean into the latch with everything I have until it gives way with a gritty scrape, almost sending me tumbling butt over braids.

Cub pulls and I push Dead End into the stall. Inside it, he whimpers and looks up at me with huge, questioning, chocolate-brown eyes. "Only for a minute," I whisper as I close the door. "For the love of steak bones, be a good dog. PLEASE!" Thank goodness he isn't much of a barker.

"The shampoo and towels!" Cub dives at the tin tub and turns it over on top of them. He grabs the spit-wet bone and tosses it under the tub.

The barn door hinges squeal. The bailing twine Cub has been working with unravels as G.D., as thin and bent as a willow branch, pushes the door open and steps inside. Years ago, when Mom and I had started our

9

game of picturing people as animals, we'd labeled him a mountain lion. But he's shrunk since then. A cold twang shoots through my chest as I wonder what animal Mom would see him as now.

"Phew! This Virginia summer is sizzling like butter in a hot frying pan." G.D. leans on the plain, dark wood cane that he got from some antique dealer in New York. That dealer swore the cane had belonged to a Civil War captain and that the round top had come from a melted-down rebel cannon. No wonder the thing became irresistible to G.D.

"Knew I heard someone out here." He pushes up the brim of his tan cowboy hat—another souvenir, this one from Texas, that I've seen a million times during all his visits over the years. It had once fit him as snug as a sock, but when G.D. came to live with us nine months ago, to help Lyon and me take care of Mom, I'd noticed that either G.D.'s hat had swelled or his head had shrunk.

"What are you two magnets for trouble doing in this old dust trap of a barn?" He smiles, his sky-blue eyes getting lost in the creases of his tanned face—a map of his seventy-two years.

My heart almost thumps through my chest as I glance at Cub, who is making himself as tall as a short kid can while stuffing the bottom of his oversized T-shirt into his shorts. Mrs. Bayer has trained her boys to always look neat and be respectful around adults. The world could be ending, but they'd be tucked, buttoned, and zipped.

I look back at my granddad, and try to force a return smile. "Not doing much of anything," I squeak.

Already Cub's cheeks are giving us away, turning blotchy red, the way they do whenever he gets to feeling guilty.

G.D. follows his cane into the shade. "Was on my way to the garden when I heard you two out here." He says he can hear me from anywhere. *This comes from you and me being closer than two tomatoes on the same vine,* he's told me more than once. "Seeing what you weasels were up to seemed like a better idea than pulling up weeds." He chuckles at calling us weasels, but his grin dries up quick. "Why are you tugging on your braids, girl?" He squints hard at me. "What are you nervous about?"

Dead End whines and scratches. I slam my back into the stall door to hush him.

G.D.'s expression flattens. "What's going on here?"

Dead End whimpers and scratches some more, spattering dirt out from under the stall door and onto my riding boots.

"What the . . ." Stiffer than rusted metal, G.D. hobbles over to me. "Step aside, girl."

"Party's over," Cub mutters under his breath.

My heart pounds hard enough to bust a rib, but I do what G.D. tells me to do.

When he peers into the stall, his eyes go wide. "Well, dress me in a gown and call me Cinderella. What's my favorite dog doing out here? And what in all of creation has he rolled in?" The latch scrapes as G.D. works it. The minute the door swings open, Dead End jumps out as if he has springs in his legs, his tail swinging like a furry windshield wiper. Grinning, his nose caked in dirt, he leaps in circles around G.D., the happiest pooch in the world. Even the shade of the cowboy hat can't hide the way G.D.'s face crinkles into a laughing grin.

Cub steps back to keep from getting plowed. "Dead End sure is glad to see you, Sir."

"He's my buddy." G.D. leans on the cane to lower into a squat. Then he strokes the dog's face, slow and tender, and wipes dirt off the pooch's nose, the black of it worn pink down the middle. G.D. says this scrape shows the dog has dug himself out of more than a few places in his time—before Mom taught him how to be a good dog.

G.D. straightens. "Where's he been?"

I hesitate, not sure how to answer.

"He's been gone since yesterday morning, Sir," Cub says, opening his big trap.

"What?" G.D. turns to us, his face holding his question. "I wondered why I didn't see him nosing around at dinner last night. When did he come back?"

I shrug, grab Dead End's leash. "About an hour ago."

G.D. blinks back his shock and surprise. "Does your pop know about this?"

"Lyon's been coming home too late to notice anything," I mutter. *And he's been leaving before the sun comes up*, I don't add because we both know this well enough.

G.D. shakes his head. "Taking off. Sounds bad, but I'm sure there's a good reason for it." He bends over, runs his palm down Dead End's back. "Hope so, anyway. Your pop won't tolerate this dog running around and pestering folks again."

"He's only run a few times since . . ." I stop, refusing to speak any words that fire up the hurt I've been keeping inside—a pain big enough to suffocate me. Instead, I imagine stuffing all my ache and sadness into one of the canning jars that Mom used to put cucumbers in to make her famous bread and butter pickles. I picture my hands screwing the jar lid tight the way she'd taught me to do, then storing the container down deep inside myself the way we'd put those pickle jars in the basement, to ferment.

G.D. tips his head from side to side, studying the dog. "Where'd these stains come from? What he's been doing?"

Cub pulls his T-shirt back over his nose. "He stinks bad."

"Manure." G.D. squints at the greenish brown–soaked fur. "Cow or sheep."

Cub pokes an index finger at the sticky, darker stains under Dead End's chin and on his muzzle. "That isn't any kind of manure that I've ever seen."

The pooch drops his head, guilt in his eyes as he turns his face away from us. Mom always swore the dog could understand simple English.

Sadness settles like dust from the garden in the wrinkles of G.D.'s face. "Blood. Those dark stains are blood."

"Ahh—gross!" Cub smacks a hand over his T-shirt-covered nose. "I might throw up."

Maybe a some-day veterinarian shouldn't get so sour at the sight and smell of blood, but the raw stench coming off Dead End does seem ten times more disgusting once labeled. Even I stagger back from the dog. "Bet he got into a deer carcass in the woods," I say.

"Better hope so." G.D. turns and hobbles back toward the barn door. "Because bloodstains are a bad sign. They tell me . . ." He stops short, winces and grips his left leg.

"G.D.!" The alarm in my voice bounces off the barn walls.

Cub leaps at him.

G.D. waves him off. "I'm all right." He rubs his left thigh. "Dang leg."

Dead End whines and pulls to get to G.D., but I keep our dog close. Cub looks at me with question. *Leave him*, I mouth. G.D. asks for help when he needs it.

At the doorway, he glances over his shoulder at me. "I hope Dead End isn't going back to his old wandering ways because of your mama's . . ."

"STOP! Don't say it!" I stare at my riding boots, my words hanging in the steamy air.

G.D.'s thin lips press together. His eyes turn watery. The missing-Mom look I've been getting to know. "It's been three months, girl. Time for you to start talking about what happened."

But I can't.

• • •

After G.D. leaves us, Cub goes to the barn door, begins looping twine around its latch to hold it closed, all the while keeping his eyes off mine. G.D. says Cub has horse sense, meaning he knows when to leave me be. I say he'd freeze like a deer caught in headlight beams if

I let go any tears. Because he knows what I fear most: that if I start crying, I might not stop.

"Dill, what if G.D. tells Lyon that Dead End's been takin' off again?"

My belly rolls over at the possibility. "I don't know, Cub. I really don't know."

CHAPTER 2 GONE

"THE SECOND YOU FINISH MUCKING THE STALLS and I finish riding, we'll give Dead End that bath. In this heat, he'll dry and be back inside the ranch before Lyon misses him," I say, as Cub and I step into Ms. Tucker Hunter's riding stable. Already Crossfire is nickering, and pushing at his stall door, tossing his head. I love this spunky liver-chestnut horse with the white stripe dribbling down his face, maybe because I ride him in shows or maybe because I always rode him when Mom, Lyon, and I took horses out on the trails. Those were happy Saturday mornings filled with Mom's laughing and Lyon's whistling.

"Crossfire knows we're late," Cub says, an edge to his tone because he hates being late.

"Or he smells the carrots you brought." Cub always brings garden vegetables for Ms. Hunter's horses and goats. Not because he rides. Cub has zero interest in climbing up and onto a horse. He simply adores animals and likes to spoil them. He'd work here for free just to be near them.

"Hey! What're you two doing?"

The loud and too familiar high-pitched demand freezes Cub in the middle of pulling a carrot from his back pocket. Crossfire throws his head up, spooked. Jerry Smoothers, the best riding instructor at Ms. Hunter's stable, but also the grumpiest, stands at the end of the aisle with his hands on his hips. Ms. Hunter told me once that the accident that ended his career as a jockey had soured him. *Too much disappointment in one lifetime,* she'd said. *But he's not as mean as he seems,* she'd added. *Did you know that he spends his free time trying to find homes for lame and retired racehorses?* According to Ms. Hunter, no one loves and understands horses better than Jerry Smoothers. He just loses his patience with people.

And there's plenty of that impatience coming off him now. His tight-lipped frown and dark, slicked-back hair highlight his mean streak. Mom used to peg him as a rat, but I've always seen him as pure snake.

His riding boots stomp in uneven steps right up to Cub. Jerry's anger, like his limp, is a kind of scar. "Dameon Thornburn is missing his crop."

My jaw tightens as I struggle to keep from saying *And he's blaming Cub and me for taking it, right?*

Because Dameon Thornburn lives to get us in trouble. Six months ago, he blamed Cub for cutting up some new saddle. But since everyone knows Cub wouldn't slice an apple that didn't belong to him, this led to nothing but Dameon's parents buying him another saddle and Jerry Smoothers holding tight to a fistful of doubts about all of us. The man doesn't trust anyone between the ages of five and twenty.

Truth is, Dameon sliced his own saddle. Because he got a bur in his briefs over Cub and I not including him in our hayloft jump, when Cub hung a rope from the rafters in the stable loft and I showed everyone interested how to swing out and drop into the hay. The kind of fun that scares the pants off Dameon. And when this kid gets scared, he goes whining to his mother. This always lands Cub and me in a pile of trouble with Jerry, who ends up having to calm Mrs. Thornburn—a woman who shrieks when she gets mad.

The fact that Ms. Hunter likes Cub and me and lets me ride her horses in shows—not to mention how I always place higher than Dameon in them even though his parents bought him one of the finest horses in the state of Virginia—established his sour attitude toward us long ago. Cub says Dameon thinks he's entitled to friends and blue ribbons simply because his family has more money than the earth has dirt.

Also, Cub nicknaming Dameon *Skeeter,* short for *Mosquito,* annoys the spit out of him. Apparently, Dameon doesn't agree that he can be more irritating than fifty of those insects plus ten. *He thinks people were put on this earth to serve him,* Cub is always telling me.

Cub's dad, the minister, says Dameon is jealous of our friendship. The minister thinks we should reach out to the Mosquito. Cub says he'd reach out to a rattlesnake first. Mom used to describe Skeeter as insecure. I describe him as a flat-out jerk.

Jerry whips a stiff finger at Cub's nose. "Why does Dameon think you two took his crop?"

Because he's a freak, I itch to point out. "Don't know," I do say, trying to sound sweet and innocent. Ms. Hunter listens to Jerry. Getting on his bad side means risking my job and all that goes with it: the pay, the free riding lessons, the horse shows.

"If we find that crop, we'll be sure to tell you or Ms. Hunter." I pour on the sugar.

By some miracle, Cub doesn't choke on this.

Jerry squints hard, looking from Cub to me. "I've seen how you and Dameon Thornburn treat each other—mean." He grunts, sounding disgusted. "You kids got no idea how to treat others. No respect."

"Yes, Sir," Cub mumbles.

But Jerry keeps scowling at us. "You two better not let me catch you with that crop. The minute you cause trouble, I'll smell it. I promise you that."

Twisting the bottom of his T-shirt into a rope, Cub focuses on his crusty, unlaced work boots with the hole wearing through the right toe. "Yes, Sir. I mean, no, Sir. I mean, you won't catch us doing anything, Sir. . . . I mean, other than work."

Jerry leans toward me, his eyes still slits. He aims his rigid pointing finger at my face. "One wrong move, Dylan MacGregor, and I'll make sure you don't ride Crossfire or any of Ms. Hunter's horses in the regional show."

"Of course," I say, knowing Jerry Smoothers is as good as his threat.

Even after he snarls something about snot-nosed kids and stomps off, Cub and I stand still as stones for a minute that feels like a millennium.

"Skeeter's settin' us up, Dill," Cub finally says low. "He knows you'll beat his sorry butt at the regional show. He'd kill to have you scratched from it and both of us fired."

"He can't prove we took anything of his." I head for the empty stall where Cub and I last left the wheelbarrow and pitchforks.

"He needs a crop where the sun don't shine," Cub mutters, sounding like his big brothers, Timmy and

Jimmy, the twins who get into more trouble than a pair of tomcats.

Before I can say anything else about Skeeter, the door at the front of the barn slides open. I turn halfway around to face it and almost head-butt Cub. Short and stocky Mr. Bob Kryer, who Mom and I labeled a bulldog, storms inside, almost plows over Jerry Smoothers.

"Jerry!" Mr. Kryer sounds rushed and tense. His voice, thick and wet from his stuffed nose, echoes over the stalls. The man sneezes, sniffs, and drips his way through most summers because he farms hay even though he's allergic to it. "Where's Tucker? There's a big problem over on Barley Lane. Dogs attacked Jim Wilson's sheep this morning. The sheriff asked me to warn everyone with animals."

"What? Attacked? How?" For once, Jerry Smoothers sounds stunned instead of angry.

Before Mr. Kryer can answer, the office door near Cub and me opens. "Hey, Dill. Hey, Cub," Ms. Tucker Hunter says in a cheerful, sort of singing tone, smiling at us. Tall and plain and as sleek as one of her show horses in her riding breeches and boots, she steps into the aisle and turns to the men. "Hey, Bob, Jerry." As usual, her tone is friendly, but holds authority. She takes long strides toward the men, her red ponytail, as long and as thick as a horse's tail, swings against her back. "You gentlemen look much too serious."

"Dogs attacked Jim Wilson's sheep early this morning, Tucker." Mr. Kryer wipes his knuckles under his thick nose, then pulls out a cotton handkerchief and blows into it.

Ms. Hunter goes stiff and straight.

"Those poor sheep," Jerry says to no one in particular.

Cub grabs hold of my arm. "Dead End was out until nine this morning," he whispers.

Mr. Kryer sniffs, focusing on Ms. Hunter. "According to Jim, those dogs chased and cornered a sheep. Then one of those mutts went for the sheep's throat. Killed it."

The word *killed* plows into me like a freight train and makes me gasp. Cub glares at me in a warning to shush.

One of Ms. Hunter's hands goes to her chest, over her heart, while her other hand goes to the cell phone at her waist. I'm guessing she's wanting to call someone, anyone, about this killing. She loves animals as much as Cub and I do, as much as Mom had.

"Dogs." Jerry whistles high and long, the way he does when a horse does something crazy and unexpected.

"The sheriff's on a rampage," Mr. Kryer adds. "Says he's seen dogs come together in a pack and start to kill like wolves. He says once they taste blood, it's almost impossible to stop them. People's animals, whether pets or sources of income, are in danger."

"Did Jim see any of these dogs?" Leave it to Ms. Hunter to ask the very question that is rattling around in my head.

"Thought he saw a black lab."

"Pete Crowley has a black lab," Jerry Smoothers snarls.

Cub makes a choking sound. He adores that dog, takes care of Blackie whenever the Crowleys put their mobile home on the road. Mr. Pete Crowley even offered Cub one of Blackie's pups once, but Cub's father said the Bayers already had too many bellies to fill. When Cub suggested getting rid of a few of his brothers to make room, he almost got grounded for life.

As Ms. Hunter and the men walk away from us, Mr. Kryer keeps shaking his head and sniffing. "Jim said the dog that went for the sheep's throat looked familiar." The group turns a corner. Mr. Bob Kryer lowers his voice, but I can still make out his snuffled words. "A blond husky. And he thought he saw that mutt again a half hour ago. Thought it might be the MacGregor's dog, but it took off before he could get a good eyeful of it." Mr. Kryer sneezes again. "I told Jim to make sure he recognizes the dog before he accuses anyone. Lyon, Dill, and her grandfather have enough heartache these days."

"Blond husky!" Cub practically spits into my ear as the voices fade. "That could be Dead End!"

"I don't care if Mr. Wilson saw a *pink* husky," I snap. "Dead End's locked in the barn. You rigged the door shut yourself. Remember?"

Cub's face goes red.

"Come on." I start toward the sliding door. "Let's go check on him."

"What about mucking out the stalls?"

"We'll come back here as soon as we make sure Dead End is in the barn." Being a good dog, I hope.

• • •

I bust into the old barn so fast that I near trip over Dead End's rawhide bone. But the hollowness of this place without Mom's animals stops me. Seymour, the one-eyed goat adopted by Mom three years ago when no one else wanted him, should be trotting over to me to nibble on my clothes. Double and Trouble, the brother and sister cats that Mom called her rambunctious teenagers, should be wrestling and chasing each other. The lop-eared rabbits, Romeo and Juliet, should be butting at the hutch door, looking to come out.

"Dead End? Here boy!" I clap. He always comes running, his mouth open and his tongue hanging out, when Mom, Lyon, G.D., or I clap.

"He's gone, Dill." Cub examines the frayed twine that had secured the door shut, but now hangs loose and useless off the handle.

Hay rustles. Annie, one of the tan hens, darts out from behind the stacked bales. Clucking as if someone is chasing her with an ax, the chicken shoots for the doorway, moving faster than her stumpy legs should be able to go.

Cub watches her. "Old Annie wouldn't be in here if Dead End was around."

I look up into the rafters and cobwebs as if Dead End could have grown wings and flown up there. Dan, the rooster, struts across a beam. He clucks with concern, jerking his rust-colored head, his bead eye accusing me of hiding the truth about Dead End from Lyon.

I turn to the hay bales, begin pulling. "Maybe Dead End squeezed himself back here. He wedges himself behind our washing machine at the first crack of a thunderstorm."

Cub snorts his doubt. Outside, Annie keeps cackling. Above me, wings flutter as Dan drops from the rafters. The second he lands, he shoots for the door, a feathered gentleman in a clucking frenzy. I never understood why Mom loved these spastic birds.

Cub pushes the barn door farther open with his foot, exposing fresh claw marks and a new hole in the dirt floor. "Dill, he's gone."

My stomach curdles. The hot, stuffy air gets thicker and hard to breathe as my fingers uncurl from the twine of a hay bale. I wipe sweat from my face. Hay dust scratches.

Cub kicks at the claw marks. "Jeez. This means . . ."

"Don't say it!" My hands clench. That chicken clucking is about pecking through my nerves. If Cub says even one word about sheep, I'll slam him. "G.D.'s probably got the pooch." I turn, head for the ranch. After G.D. arrived and started caring for Mom, he and Dead End and Mom became almost inseparable. Until three months ago.

As I reach the garden, the door hinges at the back of the house screech. Lyon hasn't fixed much around our ranch home in the last year, since we found out Mom was sick.

"There's my girl!" G.D. steps onto the porch, adjusts his cowboy hat.

"Hey, G.D." I toss him a grin that feels fake. "Did you bring Dead End inside?"

"Nope. These dang legs have been giving me too much trouble to do much of anything this morning." He massages his left thigh. "Why?"

"No reason," I squeak.

G.D. taps down the steps, as fragile as a rusted tin man. The rings jingle beneath his white T-shirt. "How about some help in the garden, Dill?" His grin trembles as he gives his thigh a pat. "I won't be able to get to the low weeds without you today."

I glance at my bike lying next to Cub's, where we'd dropped them on the gravel driveway. Then I look back at the neat rows of green that promise enough vegetables to feed even Cub's family. Swallowing a watermelon whole would be easier than saying *no* to helping G.D. with Mom's garden. When she could no longer stand the sun, thanks to hospital treatments called *radiation* and *chemotherapy,* G.D. dug into that garden as if it was his own. Because he knew she watched him from a window. *I'd do anything for your mama,* he'd told me.

"Sure, I'll help." But I don't sound convincing. "As long as I get back to the stable before it gets too late. To muck out stalls and ride Crossfire."

G.D. shakes his head, continues toward me. "You're working too hard, girl. Cooking meals, cleaning, putting in stable time, training. Can't fool me. You're trying to dodge the hurt."

When I say nothing, focus on my feet, G.D. sighs. "All work and no play can dull a girl, Dill. I can't remember the last time I saw you with all your friends— not just Cub."

"Summer's hard." I try to keep my voice steady. "My other friends live miles away. Too far . . ." I stop, unwilling to say *to get to without Mom driving me*. And

I'm in no mood to talk about how no one feels comfortable coming to me these days. Because the ranch has lost its laughter, its warmth.

Cub storms up behind me. "I hate it when you stomp off like that, Dill."

My chest aches as I watch G.D. continue to struggle across the backyard to get to Cub and me. "He asked me to help him in the garden," I tell Cub, my voice low. "He's never asked for help with that. He prefers to do the gardening by himself." In fact, G.D. doesn't ask for help with much of anything. Lyon says this independence comes from years of G.D. traveling around the country on his own. *Solitary as an eagle,* Mom used to say. Or a mountain lion.

"Wish someone at my house *preferred* to do the gardening alone," Cub mumbles.

G.D. pauses halfway across the lawn, looking past me, at the barn. Searching for Dead End? "Cub," G.D. calls after finally breaking this stare. "Your brother Danny telephoned. Something about you needing to mow a field."

"That's *his* job," Cub growls.

Danny, second from the oldest of the Bayer boys, is always bossing Cub around.

"You can't go." My tone begs. "We've got to find Dead End."

"I have to mow," Cub grumbles.

Because his helping on his family's farm is a serious requirement, right up there with attending church services every Sunday. Even though I know this, I still itch to convince him to stay and help me.

"I'm gettin' real sick of all the chores," Cub adds. "I'm lucky my mom let's me spend as much time as I do here." Anger makes the edges of his words sharp.

She feels sorry for me, I don't point out, keeping quiet because Cub doesn't need more lip about me right now. Unlike most of my girlfriends, he doesn't complain much unless he is real bothered and needs to be heard.

As G.D. starts toward us again, I try to think of something comforting to say to Cub. "I'll look for Dead End on the way to the stable," I finally suggest, returning to my own problem, not being as good of a friend as I want to be. As Cub has been. Because my finding that pooch around here, alone, smack in the middle of farm country, promises to be harder than spotting a flea on a sheepdog.

"My years are showing," G.D. says between heavy breaths as he approaches us. "Remember how I'd hike for miles? I'd wear out three pairs of boots in one afternoon. Not anymore, though. Old age is no carnival."

A lump the size of a golfball swells in my throat. I can't take G.D. talking about getting old, fading.

"Don't worry about helping me in the garden, Dill.

I'll get Dead End to lend me a paw. That dog is good company." G.D. chuckles, looking at the barn again.

Before I can agree, G.D. squints at Cub. "Why are you getting as red as an overripe tomato, boy? What's wrong?"

I stop breathing, scared to the bone that Cub will blurt out something about dog packs and sheep. The kid can be too much like his father, the minister, always putting the truth on the table. *Cub's dad lives what he preaches,* Lyon has told me. *Got to respect that.*

"Dead End, Sir." Cub shuffles from boot to boot. "Seems he took off again."

"CUB!" Every muscle in my body itches to pound him.

One of G.D.'s bird-claw hands tightens on the cane top. "Again?" He blinks fast, focuses on his dried, cracked cowboy boots, embedded with dirt and dust from every corner of the country. His free hand rubs his thigh as he blinks his eyes, which are getting suddenly moist. He shifts his gaze to me. "Seems that dog is looking for your mama."

The stabbing ache that goes with her name, the pain I've been trying to keep in the jar deep down inside myself, swells and seeps out from under the sealed lid. It crawls up into my chest, throat, and face. I swallow in gulps, taking in big breaths to keep back tears. "Cub and I will find Dead End, bring him back," I manage to choke out. "Then everything will be great." *Everything will be great* happened to be Mom's favorite phrase. Words I used to believe when *she* said them.

"Dill, if that dog is going back to his wandering ways, something will have to be done." G.D. hesitates. His face sags.

"G.D., no. Dead End is *our dog*!" Mom's dog. She loved him so much that she drove something like three hours each way to take him to Mrs. Sarah Doyle's obedience classes.

And that thought makes me consider: Maybe Mrs. Doyle, Mom's best friend since the puppet corner at the Fairfax County kindergarten, might be able to help again. For the last three months, she has been calling every few days to check on Lyon, G.D., and me. But how would I get our dog to her? I sure can't ask Lyon to take me to Fairfax. Even if he agreed to leave his store for a day to go visit the Doyles, he'd insist on visiting the only part of the world I cannot see. Mom's new place.

G.D. shakes his head. "No wonder your mother labeled you her mustang. You're every bit as strong-willed and stubborn as one of those wild horses."

Rugged and spirited, but also enduring, she'd said. She'd been a swan: beautiful, graceful, and too delicate for country living.

32

G.D. reaches out, touches my braid. *Your hair is getting real long. It reminds me of my Betsey,* he'd told me only a few days ago. High praise.

But looking like the grandmother I never met isn't why I've vowed never to cut my hair again. Mom always cut it. Since she can't anymore, then no one will.

"Dead End hasn't gone back to his old ways," I say, even though a little piece of me wonders if this is true.

"I hope not." G.D. rubs the white stubble on his chin. "But something has gotten under his fur. Your mama, who could charm the rattle off a snake, got him to be a homebody, but now it seems he's back to being a free spirit."

He's running from what is, I don't say. "He'll settle again," I do say. "You roamed around forever." My voice wavers. "But you finally came to stay with us."

"That's different. You all needed me. There's nothing like being needed to take your mind off your own heartache." G.D. pulls his hand back from my hair before he moves toward the garden.

Whenever G.D. speaks of heartache, he means losing his wife, Bets. When she passed on, he put her wedding and engagement rings along with his own wedding band on a chain and fastened it around his neck. He sold his horse farm, gave away all he owned except his pickup truck, an old trunk, his knapsack, and whatever clothes he could carry, and took off. *Figured wandering about the country would take my mind off my misery,* he'd told me. Mom used to say that he ran from the cold loneliness of his loss. Whenever Lyon worried about this aimless wandering, Mom told him G.D. would settle down once he could be still enough to feel the heavy beats of his swollen heart.

I never understood this before, but these days I hardly get through breakfast without thinking about running, like Dead End, from the thick and sticky sadness that stains every inch of our ranch home.

"Dead End does have a mind of his own," Cub says low.

"That doesn't make him a bad dog," I snap. "Maybe it makes him a smart dog."

CHAPTER 3 | # WISHING FOR DEAD END

As I poke a spoon at the browning beef and sizzling onions, I wonder again how I'm ever going to find Dead End and haul his furry butt home before Lyon notices the dog being gone. The question sticks like gum to the bottom of my riding boot, smack next to another worry. Did I disappoint Ms. Hunter by not cleaning out the stalls first thing this morning, the way she expected me to? Sure, I finished the job this afternoon, after searching for Dead End, but Ms. Hunter wanted the work done early. She requires her stable to be run in an organized way. Upsetting her is about the last thing I need to do. Her stable is my refuge these days. The one place where I don't keep expecting to see Mom.

"Our dog could be anywhere," G.D. mumbles from his seat at the kitchen table, more to himself than to me.

"I'm sure he hasn't gone far," I say, picturing the dog sitting and panting near Mom in this very kitchen while she cooked or baked, both of them smiling and happy.

"The last time the pooch took off, Cub and I found him in the woods behind the stable." I try to sound upbeat. *But the dog wasn't there this afternoon,* I don't add. "He's just confused right now."

"Like you?" G.D. squints hard at me. He's always been able to sense my inner troubles.

I give him my *I don't want to talk about me* look.

"And you've been running around all day. So, why are you making dinner when we got a freezer full of casseroles, fried chicken, and covered dish meals?"

Because filling the ranch with Mom's cooking brings her close again, I don't say. Being in this kitchen, her room, makes me feel like she could walk in here at any second. That everything could go back to being happy and as it should be. And because I think Mom would want me cooking her recipes. I always watched her cook, helped her gather ingredients, and measured for her while we talked about school, friends, and riding.

At least until she got down-and-out sick, and meal-making times became bed-sitting times, with me doing most of the talking and Mom listening, sometimes with smiles. Dinners became unimportant then, turning into frozen pizzas, canned soups, and cold cereal.

"I see what you're doing," G.D. scolds. "You're avoiding what's happened."

I start to chop peppers, hammering the knife hard. "Maybe it just annoys the spit out of me how everyone within a five-mile radius has been bringing us meals for the last three months." As if casseroles can plug the gaping holes that Mom has left. "Why does everyone think I can't cook any better than Lyon?" A guy who finds boiling water a challenge.

"Folks want to help, girl. That's all." G.D. lets out a long breath. "Okay. If you insist on cooking, let your old granddad help." But he winces as he tries to push himself up from his chair.

I wave him back down. "You're helping me plenty from where you are." I try to sound cheerful—for him.

I'd never admit it, but cooking dinner does seem like a waste of time tonight, since Dead End has taken our appetites with him. And I'm sure not cooking for Lyon. He hasn't shown up for even one sit-down dinner since Mom left. He'd rather stuff down leftovers after midnight—or whenever he drags himself back to the ranch after work. Mom could always get him to come home for dinner, but not me.

"Got that chili recipe from a hitchhiker in El Paso." G.D. eases himself back into the chair. "Gave it to your mama. She knew what to do to make it better than delicious." G.D. shifts. "I miss everything about that woman." He stares at his boots. "Never met anyone who loved dogs more than me, until Lyon brought her around."

I concentrate on chopping more peppers. "I added extra beef, to put weight back on you."

G.D. rubs his chin. "Don't count on that. But I'll eat my share. You're a darn good cook. Take after your mama."

I smile. Compliments like that are sweeter than fudge, especially since I wonder if Mom had been teaching me to cook to get me ready to take her place in the kitchen.

"If I were a betting man, I'd wager that you'll be as long-legged and pretty as your mama, too."

Now I really smile.

"You're a good combination of your parents."

I've heard this before, but these days it gives me special comfort.

"Got your love of horses and your riding skills from Lyon and me. My boy has always been a top-notch rider. And he gets such a kick out of watching you ride."

My smile goes flat. "You mean *used to*." I return to the browning beef and stab hard at it. "Lyon doesn't go near the stable anymore. Not to watch me ride. Not to ride himself. Whenever I ask him when we'll ride again, together, the way we used to do, he says he's too busy at his stupid store."

G.D. nods in that knowing way he has. He's told me before that Lyon escapes to MacGregor's Feed and Farm Store to keep busy while absorbing what has happened.

"Even Ms. Hunter's been asking about where he's been," I mutter.

Good thing she doesn't hold Lyon's disappearing act against me. She still pays me to feed, groom, and exercise her horses, still gives me free riding lessons and lets me ride Crossfire in shows. G.D. figures Ms. Hunter likes that I make her horses look good by winning blue ribbons. Lyon says she respects how I put away my pay, saving for my own horse or even my own stable someday. Mom used to say that Ms. Hunter was simply a smart woman who recognized a hard worker and fellow animal lover.

But I wonder if Ms. Hunter has noticed how my heart has wandered away from its one-time focus on show rings, blue ribbons, and shiny trophies.

"Your pop can't be around the horses right now, or the smells of grain and leather," G.D. says, his voice low. "They remind him of happier times."

I stare at the chili. "All he does is work. He hasn't touched his guitar, whistled, or sung so much as half a note in the last year." Even though the man couldn't hold a tune if it had a handle, I miss his singing the most. I miss sitting beside him, watching his fingers work the guitar strings as they guide his voice through a song. *He's hiding behind that wall he's been building around himself,* I don't say, remembering what I've overheard Cub's mom tell the minister. Ever since, I haven't been able to shake the image of Lyon behind stacked stones as tall as an oak tree.

My fingers find my right back pocket, where I keep the picture of Mom and Lyon that I'd laminated last week. I love this photograph of them on their wedding day—young, dressed up, polished. If their smiles had been any bigger, they wouldn't have fit in the photo.

G.D. grunts, shaking his head. "Your father's been burying himself in his work to escape the reality of . . ."

"Don't!" I jam my thumbs into my ears. After a minute of G.D. not moving his lips, I uncork my fingers, breathe. "Maybe Lyon doesn't want to be around *me* anymore."

G.D. lets a huge sigh go. "It's not you." He shifts in his chair, massaging the necklace rings. "Believe me, girl. It's not you. Your pop's trying to keep from thinking about your mama. He's running from his grief. Like you're doing with all your work at the stable and all the laundry and house cleaning you've taken on around here." G.D. glances at the refrigerator. "And all the cooking." He sighs again. "Ten people couldn't get as much done in one day as you've been doing."

After a long, silent minute, he clears his throat. "Has Cub called?"

The desperation behind his question makes my chest ache worse. I shake my head *no*. "But he's got tons of chores that keep him from a phone," I say even though I know Cub would have called if he'd seen Dead End. Before I can spit out another excuse, driveway gravel crackles. The rumble of Lyon's truck fills the garage.

G.D. and I exchange arched-eyebrow looks of disbelief as Lyon's work boots thump across the family room and enter the kitchen.

"Well, take my lunch and call me hungry," G.D. says, grinning big. "Nice to see you home at a decent hour, son."

"Yeah, I know," Lyon grumbles over the toothpick that pokes out from between his lips. He'd almost started smoking again, a year ago, when the doctors told us that Mom was sick, but she'd made him promise that he'd never go back to tobacco. Instead, he chews through forests of toothpicks.

"I'm making dinner," I tell him, sounding too hopeful.

"Smells good." But he throws me a weak half smile that tells me he won't be sticking around for dinner. I can almost hear him say *I'm sorry, kiddo*—words he used to offer up whenever I got sad or disappointed, words that always made me feel better. Almost as soon as that half smile appears, though, it disappears. Faster than a shy rabbit.

Lyon thumps to the counter where we keep the mail. "I can't stay." Charcoal crescents hang like hammocks under his bloodshot eyes. Shadows that weren't there a year ago. But then, a year ago, before Mom started going to the hospital for treatments, his black hair hadn't been edged with so much gray.

His latest toothpick slides to the opposite side of his mouth as he flips through envelopes. "I left some orders here, need to get them back to the store."

Of course he does.

"Where's our favorite dog?" Lyon glances right, and then left, his gaze pausing on Dead End's rumpled fleece dog bed lying neglected in the kitchen corner.

"With Cub," I spit out as if lying is something I do every day. "He took him for a long walk."

Lyon's forehead crinkles, probably from confusion since Cub has never taken Dead End anywhere without me. But Lyon leaves my lie alone, doesn't poke holes in it. A year ago, he'd have picked up on this fib in a hummingbird's heartbeat. Because he knows me inside and out. But he's stopped paying attention to what I do, or stopped caring.

Shaking his head, G.D. looks away from me, grumbling his disapproval. "Sarah Doyle called again," he tells Lyon after a minute that feels more like a week. "She wants you to get back to her."

Lyon gives me a smug look that I've come to hate worse than canned peas. It says, *You and I both know why she's calling.* Then he tips his head down, as if focusing on me over the top of glasses, and silently asks, "You ready to go visit your mom's place under the dogwood tree yet, Dill?" He's thrown this question my way too many times already in the last three months. It always makes me tight. And my continuing refusal to go within ten miles of Fairfax County makes Lyon tight. I'd like to say that this makes us even, but it only makes me miserable. Before Mom got sick, Lyon and I went everywhere together.

"Why don't you both visit the Doyles this weekend and . . ." G.D. pauses before hitting the issue smack in the center. He glances sidelong at me as I get ready to cram my fingers into my ears.

"Sounds good to me," Lyon says. "We'll go see where your . . ."

I mutter a solid "No" that cuts him off.

With a sigh that shows I'm exhausting him, Lyon flips more envelopes. "Apparently, Sarah Doyle and I are going to need a tow truck to drag Dill to Fairfax."

I clear my throat. "I'm making G.D.'s southwestern chili," I tell Lyon, hoping to change the subject while also tempting him into staying home. "I made cornbread, too, with corn off the cob mixed in. The way you like it." The way Mom always made it.

Of course, he keeps sorting stupid envelopes. "I'm sure it's delicious, Dill." Lyon drops the remaining mail on the counter. "Maybe I'll have some when I get home tonight." Before I can offer up an argument, he turns to G.D. "How you feeling, Pop?"

"Never mind me. What's the latest with that new store?"

Also known as the threat that's been at Lyon's back for a year and a half. Before life got serious around here, Mom and Lyon would talk about this new store for hours, working out ways to keep customers coming to MacGregor's.

Lyon wipes his hand over his eyes and bites down hard on the toothpick. "It opens next week. A huge warehouse of everything a farmer could ever need. All computerized and high-tech. Don't know how my little store will compete."

"Horse wings and hoof feathers." G.D. sweeps his bony hand as if brushing away Lyon's concern. "No one in his right mind would give up doing business with you. You're honest and hardworking. You understand farm life and the needs of farmers."

"Thanks, Pop. Now forget about my problems and tell me how your legs are today."

"They're still attached to my body. That's all you need to know," G.D. snaps.

Lyon glances at me, his dark eyes questioning. Much as I want to explain G.D.'s sour mood, I sure can't say anything about Dead End being gone. "His legs have been bothering him," I point out instead.

"Don't be troubling your pop about my legs, girl." G.D. wags a bony finger at me. "Go add those peppers and beans to the beef before it cooks into shoe leather."

Lyon sighs. "Pop, I called Doc Kerring and told him about your weight loss and leg cramps. He wants to see you."

"Send him a photo," G.D. barks.

I cringe, hating how G.D. and Lyon fuss at each other, which they've been doing forever. Mom used to say that they were like male elk crashing their antlers together—all noise and nonsense.

"You need to see a doctor, Pop," Lyon says.

I flinch, waiting for the next crash.

"I need a doctor like I need a hole drilled in my head." Straining, those creases at his eyes and mouth

45

pinching, G.D. pushes himself up from the chair. "Dill's chili will need a kick. I got hot pepper sauce from Mexico in my trunk."

"I'll get it." Lyon, as big as a bear, the way G.D. used to be, stomps past me in only two strides. "I made you an appointment to see Doc Kerring, Pop."

G.D. leans on the chair as he gets his cane under him. "I can get the pepper sauce. Go cancel that doctor appointment before I give *you* a kick. Then sit down and relax, boy. Have some of Dill's chili."

G.D.'s cane taps along the short hallway from the kitchen to the back room that he's been calling his for the last nine months, since he came to live with us. According to Lyon, soon after he married Mom, G.D. became a second father to her. And that's why he was pretty much the only person she'd let take care of her when the treatments made her weak.

Now, Lyon sighs and drops with a thump into his usual chair at the kitchen table, the one across from Mom's chair, which no one sits in these days. He adjusts the toothpick. "That man's more stubborn than a pack of mules."

"Guess that's where you get it from." I force a smile, hoping this will lighten him up.

He tries to grin at my little jab, an echo of how we used to be, always tossing teasing and grins back and forth, but now his mouth only wobbles before going flat. He just doesn't have any play in him anymore.

"He seems real down tonight, doesn't he?" Lyon looks at me then, his eyes full of the familiar bloodshot sadness. "He needs to see Doc Kerring."

I pick up a knife, start chopping more peppers. "You sticking around, having dinner with us, would be the best medicine." I never speak to Lyon like this, but he's sparked that anger deep down inside me again by talking about the doctor. Not that I have anything against Doc Kerring. He delivered me, treated all my ear infections, and stitched me up more times than anyone could count (I fell out of trees a lot before Lyon introduced me to horses). But doctors mean trouble. Lyon should know this.

He focuses on his boots, kneads his forehead. "I know it's tough seeing G.D. sick."

"He's not sick!" The words shoot out of my mouth, sharper than I mean them to be. I throw the peppers into the pan, stir them so hard that pieces of beef fly out, land in *splats* onto the counter.

"Dill, Doc Kerring needs to get a look at G.D." Lyon pauses. "You might as well know that he may want G.D. to go to the hospital for some tests."

I glare at Lyon over my shoulder. He knows that even the thought of a hospital and tests scrapes the insides of my ears, sours my stomach. "No." My voice busts out loud and startling. I turn back to the chili, grabbing a can of beans and the electric can opener. "He's not going to any hospital," I remind him, my throat tight, restrained. "He promised me that he wouldn't."

"Dill . . ."

The grind of the can opener chews up Lyon's words.

When it finally stops, he clears his throat, sounding impatient. "Dill, I know it's been a rough year, especially the last nine months, but you have to deal with . . ."

My hands slam the can to the counter. The thud is startling. My heart is galloping. Beneath it, sadness escapes the jar deep in my core. The ache swells up and wraps around my insides until my breathing becomes short and ragged.

"Dill, you can't spend the rest of your life avoiding certain words. You can't keep avoiding visiting her grave."

"STOP!" My scream about shakes the ranch as my fingers torpedo into my ears. A tidal wave of a sob wells up into my chest.

My legs take me out of the kitchen, through the family room and back doorway. I fly across the yard, wishing with everything I have that Dead End has come home.

CHAPTER 4 | NEIGHBORS AND FARMERS

T HE SWEET SMELL OF FLOUR, MILK, AND EGGS NEAR knocks me flat as I step into the kitchen. It's the first time in a long while that I've smelled breakfast when I haven't cooked it. G.D. has never gone near ovens. And Lyon hasn't opened a carton of pancake batter in months. Up until now, I figured he'd forgotten how to use a pan, and wouldn't recognize a spatula if it slapped him between the eyes. But delicious smells don't lie.

"Morning, girl." G.D. leans on a counter, winks at me.

I smile at him as the breakfast smells take me back to special times when Mom, Lyon, and I began each day together around the kitchen table, G.D. joining us whenever he visited. Mom used to say how she loved starting her day watching Lyon and G.D. smile and listen to me chatter like a mockingbird gone amuck while we all inhaled her amazing blueberry, banana, or chocolate chip muffins—made from scratch, when Lyon didn't pour pancakes.

When Lyon went to work and I went to school, or off to ride at the stable, G.D. and Mom would sit longer, drinking coffee and talk, talk, talking for hours, especially after Mom got sick and found it hard to get up the energy to garden, clean the ranch, and take care of her animals.

Even now I still catch myself half-expecting to see her by the stove, her long hair piled on top of her head, the way she wore it while cooking.

"Hope you're hungry." G.D. straightens. "Lyon made a mountain of pancakes before he left for the store this morning."

"From the batter that comes in a carton, I bet." Lyon doesn't know how to make anything but pancakes from a container. Mom tried to teach him how to cook more, until he near burned the house down. After that, she didn't let him near our oven, something I used to be able to tease him about.

That's why, for the last six months, I've been the muffin baker. Mom fussed some about this, the way she did whenever I cooked or cleaned too much, saying I needed to be a kid while I could be. But she enjoyed those muffins. I could tell by the way she closed her eyes and slid into a smile as she chewed them.

I go to the counter near the stove, pull the coffee and sugar canisters out from the cupboard, and slide them back in line with the flour and tea canisters, the way they're supposed to be—have been for as far back as I can remember. As I do this, I catch G.D. watching me, so I toss him a shrug. "Lyon has been moving everything," I explain. Everything that was a part of Mom's world. "He just can't leave things the way they should be." The way she'd had them.

I pull out Mom's dark green, metal recipe box from where Lyon keeps stuffing it behind the coffee machine. My pointer finger traces the loopy script that spells out *From the kitchen of Summer Stone MacGregor*. Knowing she wrote these words on the yellowed, grease-stained index card taped to the top of the box makes the thing precious. The recipes inside it bring her back: her famous Christmas berry cookies, her secret barbecue sauce, the chocolate cake that she'd only make on birthdays. That card even has her chocolate thumbprint on it—a bittersweet fossil.

G.D. squints at me. He does this a lot lately—studying me as if trying to peer inside my skull and read my feelings like print. "When are you planning on telling Lyon about Dead End?"

When I don't answer, he shakes his head real slow. "I heard you lie to your pop about Cub taking the dog for a walk, girl." He stares at me long enough to make me squirm. "You can't avoid the truth simply because you're afraid of it." G.D. lets out a big breath that sounds like worry. "Tell me, what'd you and your pop have a spat about?"

No way I'm going to share what Lyon said about the hospital.

"And don't tell me that you didn't quarrel, because when I came back into the kitchen with the hot sauce last night, I found Lyon trying to finish the chili."

I wince. "That couldn't have been pretty."

G.D. shakes his head again. "That boy was jumpier than a rabbit with fleas. But I didn't ask any questions. Not even when he stuck around, watching the back door, waiting for you. Figured time would tell me all I needed to know." G.D. goes to the oven, pulls out the baking sheet that holds the pancakes. "These are a peace offering or my name is Dolley Madison."

I start to braid my hair, as if I don't care about Lyon or his pancake offering.

"My Bets used to fuss with her hair, too, when trying to avoid something."

G.D. knows darn well that being compared to the grandmother I've never known always makes me soft.

"You and your pop and even Dead End need to get close again, Dill." G.D. uses a spatula to flip pancakes onto plates. "Take it from me: Trying to avoid the pain of what's happened won't do you a bit of good. Face your loss. Lean on each other. It's the only way to feel any better." G.D. pauses, thinks for a moment. "Your pop's scared, girl. He hasn't figured out how to handle what life has thrown at him. Like you. I've walked in those boots. I know how it feels to lose . . ."

As I'm about to cut him off, keep him from saying anything that will fire up the hurt, someone knocks on the screen door in the family room, making it rattle.

"Anyone home?" Mr. Fred Barley's gravel voice comes through the screen much as it has been doing regularly for the last two years, ever since he bought the farm that pushes up against our driveway and the right side of our property.

Mom always welcomed Mr. Barley and his chatter. G.D. said that this was because she'd never really taken to the seclusion of country life in southern Virginia. And old Mr. Barley always brings information, local news, and gossip. Still, his visits weren't enough. Mom drove north, back to the Fairfax County suburb where she grew up, at least once a month to stay a day or two with Mrs. Sarah Doyle. Lyon never liked this, but in the end, G.D. convinced him that Mom belonged in Fairfax. Apparently, Mom had opened up to G.D. and shared how much she missed her hometown.

"Hey, Mr. Barley." I step into the family room, ready to offer pancakes to this man who reminds me of a barrel in overalls.

"Hi there, young lady." He pulls at the visor of his oil-stained baseball cap with the tractor logo on the front of it. Part of his usual greeting. "What've you been up to?"

Before I can offer up some bland answer that might give him what he wants, his expression narrows into a squint that adds lines to his already-wrinkled and tanned face. He leans into the screen. "You been to visit your poor mother's resting place yet?"

Stunned that he'd actually asked me the question that all our other nosy neighbors won't, I go stiff. Unable to speak, I move my mouth like some kind of fish out of water. But in my head, I scream *No pancakes for you, Mr. Fred Barley!*

"Not attending the funeral, refusing to visit her grave. It's not right, young lady," he says when I don't answer him. "You need to pay respect to such a fine woman."

I don't remember asking for your opinion, I don't say, biting my bottom lip now, using every bit of strength I have to keep the hot anger inside me from spewing out of my mouth. Why can't folks leave me be? *People can be like chickens pecking at each other,* Mom once said to me. I didn't know then how right she was.

Poor Lyon, I can almost hear the neighbors pecking. *After losing his wife, his only child won't go to the cemetery. Terrible!* They don't know that Lyon brought this on himself. I told him not to take Mom to the hospital.

"Hello, Fred," G.D. calls, working his way across the kitchen and into the family room.

Good-bye, Mr. Barley, I think, itching to get away from this man, desperate to be at the stable. Being around the peaceful shufflings and shiftings of Crossfire and the other horses is the only way I can put the pecking and everything else aside, even if for only a little while.

"Came by to warn you folks," Mr. Barley announces. Rumors of trouble spread like floodwater in our community.

He pulls at the visor of his dirt-smudged baseball cap, a mangy thing that he wears day and night, probably even sleeps in. "Got myself two young steer." Mr. Barley puffs himself up, proud as a prizewinning rooster. "Wanted to warn you. Steer can be skittish."

Waiting for him to say something about the sheep-killing dog pack, I don't breathe as I watch his square face with its wide, flat nose—a steer's face.

G.D. nods. "Raising yourself some sirloin, Fred?"

He mentions top round and from there the two of them chat about beef, G.D.'s friendliness mixing with Mr. Barley's matter-of-fact farming tone. G.D. invites the farmer inside, but he says *no, thanks*. That's when I breathe again, excuse myself by mumbling something about needing to get to my riding lesson, and return to the kitchen.

I barely reach the pancakes when Mr. Barley clears his throat. "Also want to tell you that I've been made a sort of deputy sheriff," he announces without masking his pride. "Seems dogs attacked some farm animals. The farmers are having fits, are talking about getting their mitts on guns to protect their livestock. Sheriff Hawks smells trouble. He wants me to teach those farmers how to properly aim at a target before the bullets start flying."

I near fall nose-first into my breakfast.

"Say," Mr. Barley adds with too much curiosity in his voice. "Where's your dog?"

I'd have passed out if G.D. hadn't suggested, "Around somewhere."

A couple minutes later, Mr. Barley leaves and G.D returns to the kitchen. "I'm not surprised the sheriff asked for Fred's help. He's a good shot. Could shoot a can off our back fence from New Jersey if he wanted to."

I eye the big, thick pancakes. Lyon would want to know about the sheep attack, the farmers having fits about it, and the sheriff smelling trouble. Being aware of what goes on around here helps him run his store. So he'd be plenty disappointed in me for keeping information from him, especially the part about Dead End taking off.

"You owe your pop the truth about what our dog has been up to." Deep parenthesis lines crease either side of G.D.'s turned-down mouth. "Did you hear what Fred said about the dogs?"

This makes Lyon's pancakes smell a lot less sweet, much more like disappointment.

"Our dog isn't part of the sheep attacks," I snap, my tone rock-hard. "He wouldn't do that."

G.D. tips his head up and down in what I'd call reluctant agreement. "It's hard to imagine him going after livestock, but then I've been around the barn enough to know that anything is possible. Animals aren't always predictable."

"But telling Lyon the dog is gone will get that pooch a one-way ticket to a shelter."

"Okay, let's see what today brings," G.D. says. "But be careful, girl. I know what it's like to turn your back on what is. Why do you think I took off wandering like a hobo for years after losing my Bets?" His blue eyes puddle, which puts a big lump smack in the center of my throat. "Believe me, reality always catches up to you."

I don't speak. Can't.

"It's a MacGregor trait to want to burrow like a rabbit to escape trouble, but I'm here to tell you that ignoring the truth of your problems won't make them disappear. Only facing then head-on does any good."

I stare at my riding boots until the cane taps and the rings jingle back to the family room as G.D. mumbles something about how unfair life can be at times.

"Where're you going? What about our breakfast?"

He waves my questions aside. "Not hungry anymore."

"But you've got to eat!"

"I'll be in the garden." The back door squeals on its hinges, then slaps closed.

From the kitchen window, I watch him hobble across the backyard. Guilt gnaws at my stomach.

The door to the garage opens and slams closed again. "Hey, Dill." Cub's voice drags like the bottoms of his boots.

I throw myself at the kitchen doorway, almost plow over him. His clothes smell of laundry detergent and bleach. "Did you find . . . ?"

Before I can finish, he shakes his head *no*. Then he lifts his nose and sniffs, looking like a rabbit with a buzz cut. "Pancakes?"

"Never mind them. We need to find Dead End. What

if someone sees him, picks him up?" I pull harder at my braid. "What if . . . ?"

Cub's eyes go wide, showing concern. "What's got you all wound up, Dill? You drink coffee this morning?"

"Lyon noticed Dead End missing, started talking about taking G.D. to the hospital for tests. On top of that, Mr. Barley's going to teach farmers how to shoot dogs," I rattle off like some TV newsperson gone berserk while announcing headline stories.

"Shoot at dogs? Jeez." Cub scuffs his boots across the kitchen floor.

"We've got to find Dead End and get his furry butt home."

"Dill, I can't spend all day helpin' you find Dead End. Donny says I got to help the twins fix fencing in our big field. He expects me to help him in our stupid garden again, too. He says I haven't been *pullin' my weight*." Cub kicks at the floor. "I'm sick of brothers, chores, stupid gardens, and dumb vegetables. Good thing my mom likes you or I'd be home this minute helping her can tomatoes."

He should have said *Good thing my mom still feels sorry for you.*

Cub kicks at the floor. "I'm sick of Donny tellin' me what to do."

Donny, Cub's oldest brother, the tall one with the

dark eyes and hair, and the kindest smile I've ever seen. Donny sends all my girlfriends into giggles and whispers. His deep voice turns me into something like oatmeal. As much as I want to ask Cub questions, get him talking about Donny, Cub's mood screams that this isn't the time. Especially since he's never been even close to being okay with me talking about Donny. Not long ago, when I hinted at how nice Donny was after he congratulated me on a first-place ribbon I'd won in a jumping event, Cub started choking as if he'd swallowed a horsefly.

But now he keeps kicking at the floor. "I'm sick of my house. I'm sick of hand-me-down clothes, and I'm sick of too many church *functions*."

I want to tell Cub that he should be glad that he has a whole family wrapped around him, but he won't listen. He thinks I'm lucky to be an only child. He tells me he loves the peace and quiet of my home. To Cub, his house is too much like that of the old lady who lived in a shoe—the one with so many children that she didn't know what to do. He doesn't feel the hollow chill of the ranch the way I do.

"And my dad wants me to put in more hours working at the stable. Somethin' about the importance of *responsibility* and *commitment* to a job." Cub rolls his eyes. "I took that job to be around animals and make a little money, not to be responsible." He huffs. "Truth is, I'm sick of always workin'. I can't remember the last time you and me did anything fun, Dill. We haven't even been in the river this summer. And unless you're keepin' secrets, you've made none of your usual plans for cool stuff to do. By this time last year, we'd built a raft and taken it on the river, been fishin', and built that tree fort. Remember?"

"Yeah," I mutter. Cub has always relied on me to come up with ideas for entertainment. And I depend on him to make them happen. The problem is, I've lost my sense of adventure. "Okay," I tell him anyway. "After we get Dead End back, I'll help you with your chores. Then maybe we can go to the river or something."

I don't share that I'm not ready to be around his family again, all happy and whole and normal, even though helping Cub might get me Donny time because he sometimes works with us or brings us lemonade or even finishes up a job if we're tired. And always with something nice to say. Like the time he told me I was too cute to be hanging around *mangy, old Cub*. That sent my heart galloping.

"I got a riding lesson this morning, so here's what we'll do," I add. "I'll look for the pooch on my way to the stable. You look for him while you're doing stuff around your place. Then we'll meet in the barn. By then I'll have come up with more of a plan to find that dog."

"Guess that works," Cub agrees. "But, Dill?"

I glance at him sidelong, certain he's about to dump ice water on my idea.

He shifts again, looks right into my face. "What if your dog is long gone?"

Shaking my head, I turn to the window, not wanting Cub to see my eyes fill up at even the possibility. That's when I see G.D. by the garden fence, staring at the vegetables. I can almost see his hand gripping the cane tight, his thin lips pressed together, his eyes red and wet from missing Mom again. Only now, he's missing Dead End, too.

"That pooch can't be gone forever," I answer in a slipper-soft voice. "He just can't be."

CHAPTER 5 # BLOND DOGS

THE SWING AND RHYTHM OF CROSSFIRE'S WALK AS we circle the ring, cooling down after an hour lesson, and the steady beat of his hooves against the soft dirt still distracts me some, but not for long. My concentration is tissue-thin this afternoon.

"Okay, Dill, that's enough for today," Ms. Hunter calls from the center of the ring. She's standing the way she always does during a lesson, her thumbs hooked into the hip pockets of her riding pants, but she's looking disappointed as I turn Crossfire to her.

"Well, that wasn't one of your better rides," she says in a gentle voice. "Crossfire is still racing the fences. You need to hold him back and concentrate on counting the strides between the jumps. We've talked about this before."

"Yes, ma'am," I say as I swing my right leg over the saddle to dismount.

I feel her watching me, probably with those sympathy eyes that everyone keeps showing me. To avoid them,

I start leading Crossfire back to the barn, reminding myself not to run.

Ms. Hunter follows, of course. "By the way, Dill," she says as she walks up beside me and Crossfire. "Dameon tells me he's missing his crop."

My insides pucker. "I heard," I say, fighting back the urge to call Skeeter a lying pile of cow muck. Ever since Skeeter accused Cub of slicing up his new saddle, Ms. Hunter gets suspicion in her voice whenever the Mosquito's name pops up.

But now she kind of smiles, like she gets my tension and understands it. "I'm only bringing this up because I promised his mother that I would. It's an expensive crop."

"I'm sure," I mutter, holding back from pointing out that if Skeeter's mother really cared about him, she'd stop dumping him at the stable every time he annoyed her, which turns out to be almost every day. People around the barn talk about how his parents bought him a horse just to keep him busy. Even Cub agrees that this might be part of why Dameon is so hateful.

"You know I can't take sides in whatever's going on between you and Cub and Dameon," Ms. Hunter adds. "But I don't want anymore trouble around here, either." She glances at me as Crossfire's hooves clop onto the cement floor as we enter the barn. "You know, Dameon would be easier to get along with if you and Cub would include him in your activities now and again. The two of you are the only kids his age that spend any kind of time here, the way he does. I know he can be difficult, but you might keep in mind that he's bored and probably lonely."

"Yes, ma'am," I say, even though I can't see including Skeeter in anything except a thorough butt-kicking.

As we get to Crossfire's box stall, Ms. Hunter's face stretches into a warm smile. "Hey, Cub, how's every little thing?"

Perched on a hay bale, he pauses from biting off another hunk of the apple pie slab I brought him (baked Mom's way—with raisins in the filling and sugar on the pastry). "Well, ma'am. Thanks for askin'."

"Good to hear." Ms. Hunter moves on, toward her office. "Don't work too hard around here today," she adds. "It's too hot for hard labor."

She's right. The early-afternoon heat feels thicker and itchier than wet wool, and it magnifies the stable smells of sun-baked hay and sweaty horse. I slip off Crossfire's bridle, replace it with his blue halter, and then clip the aisle cross ties to it.

"Good lesson?" Always willing to help me out, Cub hops off the bale and reaches for Crossfire's bridle.

"Should have been better," I mutter. "Any sign of Dead End?"

"No." Cub kicks at pieces of hay on the cement floor. "Dill, what if he's one of the dogs that went after those poor sheep? What if we're protecting a killer?"

What if this and what if that. "He's not a killer." I release the girth, and slip the fleece pad and saddle off of Crossfire's back. Cub puts the pie down on a hay bale to take them from me. As he returns everything to the tack room, I work a brush over Crossfire's flanks, wishing I could flick off the *what if*s as easily as dust from the horse's coat.

"I can't stop thinking about that blood." Cub steps out of the room, wipes pie crumbs off his mouth with his knuckles. "Or those killed sheep."

The humidity, which is making me cranky, is keeping most people from riding. This leaves the stable quiet except for the muffled stomp of hooves on the straw-covered stall floors, the tinkling of halters, and Cub—who is also making me cranky. "I need a plan on how to find Dead End. That's all. Once he's home, everything will be great."

Riding boots clack slow and steady on the concrete aisle. "What's this about blood and killed sheep?"

I stop brushing. Cub, who has picked up the pie and taken another bite, doesn't chew. We look at each other with wide eyes, all words sucked out of us for a stunned moment. Skeeter Thornburn comes around a corner box stall, smacking his riding whip against his boots.

"Listenin' in again, Thorn-butt?" Cub eyes Skeeter's new T-shirt, so white it would probably glow in the dark, and his tailored, black riding pants. Cub has never owned anything new or tailored. Skeeter has never owned anything handed down. "Get a life." Cub spits apple and raisins. "And get lost."

Skeeter saunters toward us, his blond hair too neat, the part ruler-straight and begging to be messed with. "People who pay for their lessons and board their horses here go where they want, when they want. Not like you—the low-life hired help."

We're all in the same grade, but Skeeter goes to some fancy private school. Cub heard he doesn't have any friends there, either, which is not even close to surprising. The kid is too annoying and too mean to deal with, plain and simple.

"*Low-life help?*" Cub puffs himself up, clenches his fists. "I'll give you low-life."

I jump in front of him. Even though my being a head taller than Dameon (and a head and shoulders above Cub) makes me bold, and also makes me itch to wipe the sneer off the Mosquito's face, Cub and I don't need Skeeter's trouble. He does everything possible to get us mad, then squeals like a scared piglet when either of us gets within a foot of him. Mom used to feel sorry for Skeeter. She knew he could be sneaky and mean, but to her, he was more of a hyena pup without a pack than a mosquito or a piglet. And she'd always remind me that even the nastiest animals needed others, which is why, she'd said, Cub and I should try to include him in our fun. I still said that Cub and I should just rub his nose in dirt.

"Look, Cub." I point at the whip in Skeeter's grip. "The silver-handled crop. Didn't he whine about how it went missing? Didn't he about accuse you and me of stealing it?"

Cub squints at the engraved silver. "D.B.T.," he growls low. "Dameon-the-Bloodsucking-Tick. Yep, that's his crop."

Skeeter's knuckles go white on the whip. "At least I have a crop. You going to borrow one from Ms. Hunter for the show, Dill? You going to borrow clothes from her, too? Or is riding her horse enough grubbing for you?"

I'd pound Skeeter for this if Stubs—the big, gray stable cat missing most of her tail—wasn't creeping along the top edge of the box stall, balancing on mitten paws. Focused on Skeeter, she comes slinking up behind his head, low and slow, stalking. *She hates Skeeter,* Cub often says. *Smells the rat in him.* Cub swears that animals can sense the good and the bad in people.

I say Stubs knows Skeeter fears her, as well as every other cat on earth.

"Isn't it time for your riding lesson?" Cub stays focused on Skeeter. "Time for you to bounce all over poor Miss Velvet's back like some sorry sack of sand?"

Skeeter's eyes go squinty. "At least *I* have my own horse."

"Yeah, and you should treat her better," Cub snaps as Stubs slides closer.

Skeeter points the whip at Cub. "Tell me what you were saying about killed sheep."

Before he can say any more, a gray blur shoots at him. Two front paws thud his head, a one-two punch to his skull. With a squeal that should have blown out every eardrum in the barn, Skeeter waves his arms, spins around like a top gone berserk, and almost smacks into the hanging strip of flypaper, thick with insect carcasses.

I laugh so hard that I bend over and nearly choke. Cub laughs so hard that he nearly blows apple pie out his nose.

Stubs, her ears flat to her head, hisses at Skeeter, then drops to the floor and takes off.

When Skeeter's fancy-pants boots finally settle, he whips around and searches, his eyes wide and wild.

"Don't worry, Skeeter," Cub chokes out. "The big, bad kitty-cat's gone."

I laugh even harder, have to lean on Crossfire's shoulder to keep from falling over. Skeeter comes at me, glares over the horse's back. Crossfire tenses and pulls at the lines that attach his halter to either side of the aisle, trying to step away from Dameon.

"Stop laughing at me or I'll tell Ms. Hunter that you had something to do with those killed sheep," Skeeter snarls. "Then you can say good-bye to being Miss Favorite, Dill. You won't be riding any more of Ms. Hunter's horses in any shows."

My laughter dries up. I glare at him. "Go fall off your horse."

"Yeah, on your head," Cub spits. "You'd sell your mother's teeth to get Dill out of that show because you know she's gonna whip your butt in every event, the way she always does."

Skeeter slaps the silver-handled crop against the calf of his boots. Crossfire throws his head up, yanks toward me, and slams a front hoof onto my foot. As razor-sharp pain tears through my toes, I plant my hands on Crossfire's shoulder and push with all I have.

The second he lifts his hoof, I belly flop up, onto his back as if getting onto him to ride bareback. I grab Skeeter's collar, digging my fingers into the cotton. My braid falls forward, my glare practically drills into

Skeeter's face. "Don't EVER scare Crossfire like that again!"

Skeeter's eyes about pop out of their sockets. His hair falls across his forehead. His cell phone falls, landing with a dull thud at his feet. "Get off me, MacGregor!"

My mashed foot burns as hot as my anger, which, in these last few months, gets to boiling over any little thing. As Crossfire shifts, his head still high, his eyes so wild that the whites show, my grip on Skeeter tightens. I want to pound him, not only for scaring an animal, but for every bad thing that has happened in the last year.

"Let him go, Dill," Cub says. "Squashing Skeeter isn't worth the trouble."

"What's going on here?" The high-pitched demand and quick, uneven boot-steps can only be Jerry Smoothers.

I let go of Skeeter, slide to my feet, favoring my throbbing toes. The minute I land, I check my back pocket, my fingers searching for the photograph of Mom and Lyon. Lucky for Skeeter, it hasn't slipped out of my pocket during our scuffle.

Cub's face goes red as Jerry limps toward us.

"Dameon. Figures." Then the man squints at me. "And what are you doing, Dill?"

"Trying to groom the horse, Sir," Cub says for me.

"She tried to strangle me," Skeeter whines like the mosquito he is. "My father's a lawyer. We could sue."

Jerry Smoothers turns on Skeeter. "You're late for your riding lesson. Maybe I'll press charges for that." His squinty eyes stare hard at Skeeter, as if daring him to say more. "Go get Miss Velvet." Jerry limps off. "Lawyer. What next?"

The minute he disappears, Skeeter jabs his crop at me. I itch to stuff the silver handle up his high and mighty nose, but Crossfire jerks at the ties again.

"You wait. You'll get what you deserve, Dylan Mac-Gregor." As Skeeter stomps off, his eyes scan both sides of the aisle, probably making sure Stubs isn't waiting for him.

Mom would tell me to find the good in Skeeter. Lyon would agree, but like that I'd defended Crossfire. G.D. would say that Skeeter was the east end of a horse going west.

Cub raises his arm, aims the pie at Skeeter's head.

"Don't waste my baking on his thick skull." I stroke Crossfire's soft-as-flannel muzzle. "Give the apples to Crossfire. That idiot near scared him to death."

Cub drops his arm, picks off the pastry, and offers Crossfire the apples on a flat palm. The horse wraps his lips around them and swallows, then runs his big tongue over Cub's palm. "Skeeter heard us talkin' about the killed sheep."

Metal clinks as I unclip the ties from Crossfire's halter. "Let him think what he wants."

• • •

It's late afternoon by the time Cub and I finish up at the stable and get back to the ranch. As the door to the garage closes behind us, I imagine Dead End bounding out from the kitchen the way he always does, leaving Mom's side to greet us with his tongue out and his tail turning huge O's, his expression saying *Hey! How are ya?*

I'd do about anything to smother that dog with pets right this minute; let my fingers brush the old scar on his muzzle and the split in his ear, reminders that he once ran free as a stray, but didn't have an easy life. I'd give up my stable pay to get licks and happy dog grunts from him, to smell his fur, clean and fluffy-soft the way it always was in Mom's care. *You'd powder your chickens if you could catch them,* Lyon used to tease her.

"Hey, G.D.," I call, trying to sound perky and optimistic as I head into the kitchen and see him at the table, slumped over a spread-out newspaper. Behind me, Cub drags his booted feet. "Ready for dinner? I can make garlic fried chicken." Mom's recipe. "Or pork chops with apples. Your favorite."

G.D. gives me his disapproving look. "You don't need to be cooking again. You're wearing yourself out, girl."

I turn to the refrigerator, reach inside it for the chops and apples, waiting for him to remind me, again, that Mom wouldn't want me trying to fill her shoes.

After a silent moment, his fingers ruffle the paper. "There's not much about the dog pack in here." Then his right hand, quivering, lifts a page from beside the newspaper as he takes in a deep breath. "But we got this in the mailbox. A notice from the sheriff. He's requiring folks to register their dogs—with photographs. Immediately."

Cub goes still in the midst of tucking his shirt into his baggy shorts. "Oh, no."

I almost drop the pork. "Register? Photographs? What for? What does that mean?" If I were a building, alarms would be firing off inside me.

"The pictures will be posted on bulletin boards and the community Web site so folks can identify the dogs chasing livestock." G.D. stares at the notice. "If a dog is identified, it will be put to sleep. No questions asked. Its owner will be fined, could do jail time."

I stop breathing.

"Sheriff Hawks isn't messing around with this situation," G.D. says, placing the paper back on the table.

"That's bad," Cub mutters. "What if Mr. Wilson sees Dead End's picture and pegs him as the dog that killed the . . ." Cub slaps his hand to his mouth. His wide eyes seem to scream *I can't believe I said that!* His face goes rash-red.

G.D. squints at Cub. "What's this?"

My fingers itch to grab a dishtowel and cram it into Cub's big mouth as I stare at him, willing him to zip his lips. But asking him to swallow back the truth is like asking him to gulp down a truckload of garden vegetables.

"Spit it out, son." G.D.'s tone takes on a hard, no-nonsense edge.

Shuffling, Cub stares at his feet with wide eyes that tell me he wishes he was anywhere but here right now. He licks his dry lips. "Dill and I heard Mr. Kryer tellin' Mr. Smoothers about dogs that attacked Mr. Wilson's sheep, Sir."

"I'll make pork chops with apples," I about scream as if I can distract G.D. from Cub.

But G.D. stays focused on Cub. "What'd you hear?"

Knowing that I'm getting as tense as a mouse at a cat show, Cub glances at me. But instead of taking the hint, he sucks in a deep breath and focuses on his boots.

"Someone saw a blond husky attack Mr. Wilson's sheep. That dog killed one, Sir."

"Dead End isn't a killer!" My voice cracks.

G.D. blinks at Cub. "Those sheep were attacked after Dead End left here?"

Cub pushes a hand over his stubble hair, and shifts on his boots. "Yes, Sir."

The kitchen gets hotter, stuffier. G.D. sighs. "Then we've got to face this head-on."

My stomach feels as if it's been turned inside out. My heart thuds in jackhammer beats. "There's nothing to face. Dead End's not a killer," I say again, the anger in my throat busting out. "He's not even a half-decent watchdog. And he's never so much as snarled at the cats, the chickens, or any of our animals."

"He came home covered in dung and blood the other morning," G.D. reminds me.

"Probably from an old deer carcass!" I practically shriek.

"Listen to me, girl," G.D. states plain. "Cub just told us that a blond husky killed sheep. Our dog is the only yellow husky dog around these parts, which means . . ."

"NO!" My tone, desperate and on the edge of tears, shakes the ranch. "Don't listen to Cub. Dead End *isn't* the only yellow dog around here. That sheep-killer description fits another dog." I yank at my braid.

Cub's forehead wrinkles. He looks at me as if I've lost my mind. "What?"

"Another blond dog?" G.D.'s face crinkles with questions, but a spark of what has to be hope flickers in his eyes.

I gulp over a rock-hard lump that is now wedged in my throat. Mom used to say that a lie in your conscience feels worse than a bur in your shirt. Now I get what she meant.

"Amazing, huh?" My mouth races like a galloping horse. "Another yellow dog. Pointed ears. Big thing."

Cub stares at me, his jaw hanging open as if it has become unhinged.

Color returns to G.D.'s bony cheeks. "Where've you seen this dog?"

"Around," I squeak. "At the stable. It belongs to people on the other side of town."

G.D.'s fingers massage the rings on his necklace. "Does Lyon know this dog?"

"I'm not sure." I hesitate a second, my brain spinning. "This pooch is new in town."

A satisfied smile spreads across G.D.'s face. A bit of sparkle returns to his tired eyes and he shrugs as if to say that he doesn't know about any of this, but he believes me. "That's a truckload of relief."

"It's a load of something," Cub mutters.

My pasted-on grin pinches and pulls. I feel as fake as a puppet tied up and tangled in too many strings.

"Imagine if Lyon got caught keeping a sheep-killing dog," G.D. says. "Imagine him facing jail with everything else he's got weighing him down these days." G.D. shakes his head. "All his years of struggling to earn the farmers' trust would be lost forever. That new store would get all his business."

This about knocks the breath out of me. Why hadn't I thought about Lyon's hard work, his store, the huge new competitor that has been threatening to steal his customers?

Cub nudges my arm. "Where'd you say you heard about this other sheep-killin' dog?"

I give him a sharp look that says *Shut your mouth!*

G.D. clears his throat. "Well, that information makes me happier than a mountain lion at a pig roast, but that dog of ours still isn't home, which makes me wonder if he's gone back to his wandering ways."

"He hasn't," I insist. "Dead End is a good dog. He'll be back."

G.D. pushes away from the table, shaking his head, somehow older, more frail. "Hope you're right, girl, but I've got doubts. Serious doubts." He stands.

"Where are you going? What about dinner?" I

sound desperate, afraid. *You have to eat to keep up your strength,* I don't add.

"Not hungry," he mutters as his cane taps across the kitchen floor, to the family room.

The second the back door slaps closed behind G.D., Cub squints at me. "There's no other yellow dog, is there?"

I shrug, go to the window.

"Jeez, Dill, you lied again." Cub's voice cracks. "A big, fat lie to your granddad."

"Don't go diving headfirst into one of your dad's sermons."

Cub shakes his head. "My dad says the first lie is the hardest. Then the rest come easy." He sighs. "Dill, if Dead End is a sheep killer and the farmers find out that your dad has been keepin' him, ten million lies won't put a stop to Lyon losin' his customers."

"Everything will be great," is all I can say.

Cub shakes his head. "I don't know, Dill. I got a feeling we're goin' to be real sorry."

CHAPTER 6 | # A KILLER

"I STILL CAN'T BELIEVE YOU LIED TO G.D., DILL."
Cub's eyebrows mash together. His mouth twists down
in a disapproving look.

I kick a stone, and watch it hop over the dirt road
potholes before it pops up and into a field of tall grasses
and wild daisies. Maybe starting the day by looking for
Dead End out here, where Mom used to take him for
long walks off his leash, wasn't such a great idea after
all, especially since Cub has, apparently, decided to become my conscience. "Sheriff Hawks wanting everyone
to register and photograph their dogs is a bigger problem than some stupid lie," I mutter.

"Don't know about that."

"We can't register Dead End," I tell Cub flat out. "If
we do, he'll be accused of being one of those sheep
killers just because he fits the description of whichever
dog did go after that sheep."

"Dill, there aren't a lot of yellow, husky dogs around
here. And most folks recognize your dog."

"We could dye him." The idea drops from my mouth. Whenever Mom felt playful, she'd dye her hair some new color. Sometimes, I'd help. "There's a leftover box of Saturday Night Red in the linen closet." Because coloring stopped being fun when her hair thinned— thanks to the chemicals the doctors put into her.

Cub stops midstep and stares at me without blinking. "You gonna give the dog a perm, too?"

I roll my eyes at him, not mentioning the perms that make his mother poodlelike.

"Keep comin' up with those kinds of ideas, Dill, and your dog won't stick around long if he does come home."

I'm about to give Cub lip for cutting down my idea when he's come up with diddly in the way of suggestions, but I stop when I catch a glimpse of blond in the field to our right. "Cub . . ." I push his arm. "Did you see that?"

Halfway across the field, a yellow head with pointed ears, a long snout, and a black nose scraped pink pops up and turns to me. In the next second, the mud-splattered pooch becomes a yellow rocket shooting at us, ripping through the grass.

"Dead End!" Cub announces as if I've gone blind.

When he gets to us, his ears flatten against his head and his tail goes into wag overdrive as he leaps around me and Cub.

"Where've you been, you crazy pooch?" I drop to my knees, ruffle his neck fur, and give him pets, getting licks in return. He whips his powerful tail hard enough to dislocate his rear end, until he sees me pull his leash from my back pocket.

"He lost that collar your mom bought for him." Cub points at Dead End's neck.

"Great," I snap. "That makes this stupid leash about useless."

"Dill," Cub says in a more serious tone. He tips his head at the dog's shoulder, where the fur is matted and spiked with something thick and greenish-brown. "Manure," he says. "Sheep, probably."

"No, it's not!" I turn to Dead End, looking into those gentle eyes. "You haven't got the face of a sheep killer," I tell him. And then I drop into a squat, to kiss his scraped nose. "You're a good dog." I push my fingers through his neck fur, ruffling it. He licks my cheek, and gives happy dog grunts.

Cub melts some at this, drops beside me, and scratches behind Dead End's ears. But instead of rewarding Cub with licks, Dead End stiffens. He stops smiling. His ears go up as he looks off, down the road behind us.

Cub jumps to his feet, and puts a hand up as a visor over his eyes. "Truck! Coming fast!"

Dust billows up from the road. A loud engine rumble is moving right at us. Cub tears into the thigh-high grass. I stumble after him. "Come on, Dead End. Come on, boy," I coax him. "That's my loyal pup," I add, smiling, as he comes leaping after me.

"Get down!" Cub drops flatter than one of Lyon's pancakes.

As my knees hit the earth, my hands pat the ground, Mom's signal to get Dead End to lie down. "Sit! Stay! PLEASE!"

The engine roar seems on top of us. When Dead End doesn't drop, Cub arches up and wrestles him to the ground—seconds before a fire-engine–red pickup truck swerves around the bend, chrome gleaming. I hit the field dirt, too, getting a noseful of it.

Stroking Dead End's head, trying to calm him, Cub peers between the grass tips. "Thornburn's truck," he spits. "Thorns-in-my-butt!"

As Dead End whines and squirms, I lift my head. Skeeter's mother, an older Skeeter in red lipstick and chunky jewelry, jerks the truck all over the road, dodging potholes at what has to be ninety miles an hour. But then the truck's wheels lock. It skids to a dusty stop smack in front of us.

"Now what, Dameon?" His mother's screech echoes over the engine rumble.

Her pinched face goes hot-temper red, the way it does whenever she yells at Skeeter. Sometimes I actually come close to feeling sorry for the Mosquito.

"Dameon?" Her face tightens and twitches. "I have a luncheon to get to. You'd better not make me late!"

Cub snickers. Dead End lets loose an explosion of a sneeze. I hold my breath.

The truck door pops open. Skeeter, who's made ignoring his mother a hobby, jumps out of the truck and scowls at the field where we're hiding, his small eyes squinting and searching. As usual, he grips his stupid silver-handled crop. "I swear I saw yellow ears and a tail out there. Could be a dog."

"Don't you swear at me," his mother snaps.

"The sheriff asked me to watch out for loose dogs," the Mosquito whines. "And I think that Dylan Mac-Gregor has a yellow mutt."

"The sheriff asked *him*?" Cub growls. "A butt-kissing insect?"

Dead End whines, squirms. I stroke his face to calm him, the way G.D. does, the way Mom always did. "Please be a good dog," I beg, whispering in his ear. "Please be quiet. Please."

Skeeter waves his crop in our direction. "There's a dog in that field."

My heart races. Cub snarls "thorn-in-my-butt" again through clenched teeth.

"Dameon, get back in this truck," his mother screeches. "I don't have time for you or your nonsense." The engine revs.

A long moment passes before Skeeter does what she says. He barely slams the truck door shut behind him when gravel spatters and the truck becomes a red bullet in a cloud of dust.

I breathe only after the engine rumble fades and the dirt settles.

"Too close." Cub rolls off Dead End. The dog jumps up, sneezes again, and shakes from nose to tail, twice. "Especially after Skeeter heard us talkin' about those killed sheep."

"And like everyone else around here for five miles, he knows Dead End is a yellow dog," I add. "Exactly why coloring him Saturday Night Red is a good idea."

Mumbling something about it being more of a stupid idea, Cub heads back to the road. Dead End takes after him, leaping and nudging at his hand, looking to play. "Cub, get this leash around him somehow," I call, holding up the nylon strap.

But before I can get it to him, Dead End freezes. His ears go up. And then he bolts, becoming a yellow blur.

"Cub!"

He runs after the pooch, pointing at something small tearing through the field grass, in front of Dead End. "That dog's after a rabbit . . . or a skunk . . . or . . . *something* running for its life!"

Whatever is running from him carves a U in the grasses and throws itself onto the dirt road. There, the small, brown lump—a groundhog—scrambles as fast as its stubby legs will go. But not fast enough.

"BAD DOG! NO!" My shriek rips through the air, seeming to put everything in the world on *pause*. Everything except Dead End.

Before the groundhog gets halfway across the road, the dog leaps, lands, and sinks his face into the animal's neck. I gasp. Sickening horror and disbelief fill me up. When Dead End shakes that groundhog hard and fast until it goes as limp, I nearly throw up.

Cub waves his arms in an insane frenzy. "Bad dog! BAD DOG!" His voice wavers and cracks as if he's about to cry.

I hope with all I have that the groundhog's fur has protected him, that he's only playing dead. "Cub! Get Dead End away from that animal!"

"DROP IT!" Cub flings a rigid finger at Dead End's nose. The groundhog hits the dirt with a dull thump. Dead End, his tail plastered between his legs now, licks his bloody lips and shrinks back from his crime. He looks off to the side, avoiding Cub's glare.

"Ahh, gross." Scrunching up his face, Cub slaps a hand over his mouth and nose. He leans toward the groundhog, but quickly hops back. He fidgets, and then steps close to the animal again. He does this bizarre dance two times before he finally pushes gently at the brown lump with the toe of his boot.

The animal lays as lifeless as a log. My hand goes to my stomach where thick and putrid disgust churns and crawls up my throat. "Is it . . . ?" I can't say the word that finishes my question.

"Dead as a dinosaur," Cub says from under his hand, his face pastelike all of a sudden.

I start to shake from the inside out. A sob with roots that reach deep down wells up inside me. It takes all I have to swallow this, stuff it back into the jar, and secure the lid closed again.

Dead End's head sinks below his shoulders. Even though he refuses to look at us, guilt smolders beneath his golden eyelashes. He knows he's been real bad.

"How could you?" My voice trembles, cracking some because I understand the pain in the dog's eyes. The pain of missing what has been taken away. The pain of confusion.

And then, as if my question sends him over the edge,

the pooch bolts, tearing down the road. "Cub! Dead End!" I run after him.

Cub takes off, too. "STAY! SIT! HEEL!"

Suddenly deaf to all the commands that Mom had taught him, Dead End cuts left back into the field and rips through the tall grass and wildflowers, galloping toward a wall of trees.

Breathing harder than when he'd outrun Jeb Miller, the fastest kid in the seventh grade, Cub gives up the chase at the edge of the field. "Son of a pup," he spits after sucking in a few crucial breaths. He kicks at the road, spattering stones and dirt. "We'll never catch that dog."

I stop, too stunned to move. "I let him get away again," I choke out, wishing I could erase what just happened.

Cub whips around, and grabs his stubble hair with both hands. "Jeez, Dill! You know what his killing that groundhog means?"

"*Don't* say it!" I blink back hot, heavy tears. The question that Cub has been asking all along scratches like the point of a rusted nail: Could Dead End be a sheep killer?

Cub stomps past me, his fists clenched. "That ground-hog needs a proper burial."

I pull at the end of my ponytail. "There's no time. We've got to find Dead End. Before people see blood on his muzzle!"

Stems snap as Cub yanks daisies from the roadside. Then he bows his head over the groundhog, and drops the flowers onto the brown body. Now I know what G.D. means when he says apples don't fall far from their trees. In this moment, Cub is the spitting image of his minister father. His face is serious and thoughtful, focused. It's as if, as a preacher's son, Cub understands loss better than most and knows he needs to pay respects to it before he can accept it.

The moment becomes contagious. What Cub is doing feels right and necessary. I tip my head down. The poor groundhog. One minute here, the next minute gone. "The groundhog is in a better place," I mutter because I have to believe this. But my voice cracks. My eyes burn as drops the size of rain leak from the inner corners.

• • •

Even though it has taken us a good fifteen minutes to get back to the ranch, Cub's untied boots hit the driveway hard, full of his anger. My feet, on the other hand, stumble, full of my disbelief. My head throbs. I feel as dazed as if I'd run full out into a brick wall.

"That poor groundhog," Cub says again.

"Don't tell G.D."

Cub stops, spins around to face me, planting his hands on his hips. "Dill, the way Dead End went after that groundhog shows he's a killer. You can't keep saying he's not. You got to tell your granddad. And Lyon."

I swallow hard. What happened to our good dog? "Lyon shot a squirrel once," I say, my voice watery and unconvincing. "No one called him a killer."

Cub raises his eyebrows at me. "Dead End killin' that groundhog is nothin' like your dad huntin'."

I push past him and stomp toward the barn, hoping with everything I have for a miracle—for Dead End to be in there, chewing on his rawhide bone.

Cub jogs after me. "Dead End could go after more animals, Dill. You got to tell Lyon and G.D. what the dog did. G.D. will know what to . . ."

I whip around to face Cub. "What if Lyon gives Dead End to a shelter or has him put to sleep?" My question snaps, as sharp and as dangerous as the metal teeth of a hunter's trap. "Is that what you want?"

Cub fidgets. "No, but . . ."

"Me, neither. So, once we get him home again, I'm going to make extra sure that he stays here. No more taking off."

"Hey, you two." G.D., looking like a skinny scare-crow in his baggy overalls and the floppy white hat that some sailor in South Carolina had given him, waves a twig arm at us from the garden.

I wave back, forcing a stiff smile and heading toward him. Cub stays close.

"Hotter than the devil's workshop today," G.D. says when we get near to him. He wobbles out through the opening in the wire fencing and comes around the garden, heading toward us. When his cowboy boots hit the yard, he focuses on me while pulling a white cotton handkerchief from his pocket. He pats his glistening face. "Any sign of our dog out in the neigh-borhood?"

Even though I half expected this question, it still flattens me like a steamroller. Because I don't know what to do with it.

Cub takes a big step out in front of me and squares his shoulders. "We did find him, Sir. But he took off again."

G.D.'s smile fades. The knobby knuckles of his hand, the skin stretched like plastic wrap over bones and blue veins, tightens on the cane top. He grumbles something about how he should have known the dog would take off. "Horses will sprout wings before he'll stay home again. That's a wanderer for you." And then G.D. looks right at me. "Hope no one confuses him with that yellow sheep-killing dog you talked about, Dill."

Of course my lie would come back to bite me in the butt. "Me, too," I mumble.

G.D. sighs, and grips his cane tight. "I've been thinking, girl."

I glance at Cub, who looks about ready to bust open and spill what happened to the poor groundhog.

"There's a shelter in Utah that I know of," G.D continues.

"Shelter?" Cub goes as white as bleached sheets.

I stand stunned and silent.

G.D. lifts a thin hand in a stop signal. "This shelter's different than most. It's got acres of land. No healthy animals ever get put to sleep." He blinks, his blue eyes becoming moist. "Dead End would be safe there, wouldn't get confused with another dog and accused of anything. Only problem is, the place is clear across the country. But maybe we can find someone going out that way."

"NO! He's a part of our family!" I whine, hating this sound. "It's wrong to give family members away like old clothes."

"I'd give my brothers away," Cub mutters.

But G.D. keeps staring at me. "Give my idea some thought, Dill. Even if our dog is as innocent as a newborn pup, he could be accused, tried, and convicted simply because he hasn't been home during times of trouble."

He'll be home again soon, I don't say. He has to be, so that everything will be great again.

CHAPTER 7 | SECRETS AND LIES

AFTER DINNER, MY BIKE TIRES SKID TO A STOP ON the gravel parking lot, smack in front of the blue sign with white letters that announce MACGREGOR'S FEED AND FARM STORE. Knowing that Mom carefully painted those letters and that blue background when Lyon first opened his store makes the old wood sign special—now.

I hop off my bike and grab the brown bag from the basket that Cub has wired to my handlebars. Then I suck in a deep breath and head toward the old house that Mom and Lyon converted into the store—their baby before I came along. Mom had found it, had helped Lyon to fix it up, and had worked with him to start the business. Lyon always swore that putting her home-baked pies, cookies, and muffins on the front porch brought in the customers like fish to bait. G.D. said Mom's warm-as-sunshine smile and down-to-earth kindness kept them coming back.

For as far back as I can remember, I've helped Lyon in this store. Doing whatever he needed, sometimes just sweeping up and keeping him company. That changed though as Mom got weak and I didn't want to leave her. And then, as G.D. started tending to her more and more, I spent more time at the stable, to get away. Now, I wouldn't mind going back to the store, if Lyon wanted me to, if it didn't seem like he'd rather be left alone.

"My plan is to get Lyon to come home more by cooking his favorite dishes," I tell Cub. The way Mom did. "Tonight, I'm bringing him this garlic-fried chicken to show him that my cooking is getting better." *More like Mom's cooking,* I should have said.

"It sure smells good." Cub hums with appreciation the way he used to do whenever Mom fed him some of her home cooking. "Hope your plan works, Dill." But Cub doesn't sound hopeful as he climbs off the rusty bike that once belonged to Donny and has been passed down through Danny, Tommy, Timmy, and Jimmy.

The bell tied around the doorknob jingles as I yank the door open. Cub stuffs the hem of his bleach-faded T-shirt into his shorts, then stomps dirt off his unlaced work boots. I flick road dust from my freshly cleaned shirt, pulled from a basket of laundry I'd finished over a week ago. Since clean clothes don't lure Lyon home, I don't do a lot of regular washing and even less folding and putting away.

I've also put on flip-flops and brushed out my hair. Mom always insisted that we clean up for dinner. She'd bathe and dab on gardenia perfume. Lyon would change into a clean shirt. I'd shed my riding boots and scrub.

Standing behind the old register, Lyon lifts his head and peers at us from over the top of his drugstore reading glasses. Scattered papers, folders, a calculator, a mug stained from black coffee, and a small glass filled with toothpicks clutter the counter. Lyon still hasn't bought a computer. He says he doesn't trust technology as far as he can throw it.

"This is a surprise." Lyon sounds worn out. A toothpick pokes out from the right corner of his mouth. His face struggles to lift with one of those prepackaged smiles that he's been giving to his customers lately, free of charge. This isn't the bright-eyed Lyon who would greet everyone with big enthusiasm. That Lyon disappeared with the guy who used to sit at the kitchen table after dinner and strum his guitar.

"We brought you dinner." I hold up the crinkled, brown paper bag, the grease stain like a birthmark. I force a quivering smile, wondering if he'll figure out that I'm trying to get him to come home more, wondering if this will annoy him.

"How nice." Cement has more enthusiasm. But

when he turns his attention to Cub, Lyon seems to ease some. "How's the family, son?"

"Still too big, Sir."

"Big families can be tough," Lyon says in his *the customer is always right* tone.

I roll my eyes. Nothing could be tougher than the cold loneliness of an empty house. Lyon should know this. And since when does he think big families are rough? He and Mom had talked about me having brothers and sisters as if a dozen were on order. But they never arrived. And every time I tried to ask why, Mom's eyes got red and misty. Lyon ran here, to work more.

When Mom got sick a year ago, we repeated this don't-talk-about-trouble routine, like dance steps we'd learned by heart. Mom liked things this way. She never could take being the center of attention. But as she got thin and pale, I couldn't always keep the topic tucked away. *When will you get better?* I'd whisper as her soft hands stroked my hair. She'd tell me not to worry and then insist that I go riding or find Cub.

"Everything good at home, Dill?" Lyon pulls his glasses from his face. "G.D. okay?"

"Fine. But we missed you at dinner again. I made garlic fried chicken." The words come out stiff and awkward. I lift the grease-stained bag as I watch Lyon's expression. While I cooked this meal, I kept imagining his face getting bright when I presented it to him. I kept picturing him thanking me, maybe even hooking his arm around my shoulders and telling me that he's proud of how I'm cooking Mom's recipes.

Instead, Lyon sighs, glances at the clock on the wall. The toothpick slides across his mouth as he looks back at the bag in my hands. "G.D. had you bring dinner here?" The question is tight, tense.

I suck in a big breath. "The delivery was my idea." I focus on the counter now to keep from seeing any irritation on Lyon's face. I push papers aside, and drop the bag on the counter. "Dinners at home, with family, are important." Mom's words. She'd always insisted that we eat together at the table every night.

Lyon jumps as if startled, but then he pulls the bag closer. "Okay. You're right. I shouldn't have missed your fine meal, Dill." The lines in his sagging face seem to go deeper.

"Come home now." My voice comes out a whisper, sounding too hopeful.

He hesitates, pushes at folders. "Too much to do here."

I think about offering to help him, the way I used to do, but this feels like intruding.

Cub shifts, fidgets, kicks at the floor. "Think I'll go check out the pet stuff."

When Lyon starts unpacking the dinner without looking at me, I go after Cub. He stops near the basket of rawhide bones.

"Stay with Lyon," he spits at me in a whisper. "Tell him you need that dog, even if he is being bad."

"No! Lyon doesn't care. Didn't you just see his face? He doesn't care about anything but this stupid store. He'll get rid of Dead End the way he gave away the others." *Your mama's animals remind your pop of her,* G.D. had tried to explain to me when I fussed about losing the rabbits, Romeo and Juliet, Seymour the goat, and the cats.

Cub squeezes his lips together the way he does when trying not to lecture me. He kicks at the floor, reaches into the basket, and pulls out a bone that could have been the thighbone of a rawhide dinosaur. "*This* is worthy of your dog. Tell Lyon you're taking it, and then tell him about Dead End."

I stare at the bone, thinking that even though the rawhide he's got is big enough to choke a horse, it will take Dead End less than a day to make a slimy knot out of it, once he comes home. So I yank the bone from Cub's hands and storm back to the register.

Lyon pops the top on the plastic container that holds his dinner. The smells of garlic fried chicken and mashed potatoes mix with the store smells of grain and sawdust—scents Lyon wears like cologne. "G.D. tells me we got to get Dead End registered and photographed. Don't know when I'll find the time to do that." He sounds used up.

I place the bone on the counter with a thud. *What would happen if we didn't get the pooch registered?* I almost ask.

Lyon closes his eyes, inhales. "Mmmm. Your mom's fried chicken."

"The whole ranch smells of it," I say because Lyon always loved the way her cooking filled our home. An hour ago, the garlic and chicken had almost sent me looking for her in the family room, half expecting to find her curled around a novel, waiting for Lyon and me to clean up for dinner.

Lyon stares into the plastic container. "Did G.D. eat?"

"Lots," I say to keep Lyon from calling Doc Kerring.

Cub's jaw drops open as he stomps up beside me, staring into my face as if I've lost my mind.

Doing my best to ignore him, I watch Lyon put down his dinner to stuff the bone into a brown paper bag.

"I got to go," Cub says kind of suddenly. "There's a church thing the minister expects me to be at." The minute I glance his way, Cub glares at me. "If it's a talk about the trouble secrets and lies cause, I'll call you, Dill." Cub holds his accusing stare, being about as subtle as an elephant in an elevator.

"Say hello to your parents and brothers for me, Cub." Lyon forces another smile.

Cub stomps to the door, and pulls it open. "Yes, Sir."

When the door slaps closed, I grab the bagged bone and go after him. "I'll be right back," I tell Lyon.

When I get to Cub at the bikes, he glances at the brown bag. "Hiding the truth is as bad as lying. What if one of your dad's customers pegs Dead End as a sheep killer? Lyon will look real bad." Cub climbs onto his rusty bike. "If you want him to be a father again, you've got to be his daughter again. Tell him the truth about the dog before it's too late."

Back inside the store, Cub's words chew on me, partly because Mom would agree with them.

Lyon, a chicken leg held to his face, is chewing slowly with his eyes closed as I return to the counter. "Thanks for dinner. You make fine chicken, Dill." He opens his eyes and offers me a weary smile the way I'd offered him the garlic chicken—to take, if I want it. "It's about as good as your mother's." The weight of the sadness in his voice turns me cold. My cooking the way Mom did isn't supposed to make him more miserable.

Cub's nagging echoes in my ears like a berserk gnat.

I clear my throat, then pull at the ends of my hair. "Lyon, can I tell you something?"

"As long as it's not another problem." He seems to try harder to smile.

I must go chalk-white, because his smile slides off his face as if greased. "I'm kidding, Dill. You can talk to me about anything, anytime, as always. Don't let my mood bother you. I'm wound up about that new store. The Farmer's Outlet. It's everything a farmer could want: the latest technology, fancy merchandise, tons of stock, and low prices. Don't know how this little store will compete, especially now that folks are feeling threatened by a pack of dogs. Why shouldn't farmers go to a bigger store that offers guns and traps and more?" He sighs, sounding like a man loaded down with trouble as heavy as rocks.

Could I, should I, give Lyon another problem to carry around—a boulder with Dead End's name on it? Words stick in my throat like wads of peanut butter. "Your customers are loyal," I finally choke out, trying to convince myself more than Lyon. "They won't go to any new store."

Before Lyon can argue, the screen door swings open, the old hinges squealing. "Evening, Dill, Lyon." *Sniff.* Mr. Kryer, short and thick and sturdy as a stump, steps inside, wiping a dirt-stained knuckle under his nose. "You closed, Lyon?"

"If I'm here, the store is open, Bob," Lyon says in a strained, *my only concern is the customer* voice. The natural, relaxed tone he'd had with friends went away with Mom.

"How are you doing, Dill?" Mr. Kryer's face takes on the same dopey-eyed concern that I'm getting real sick of seeing on the adults around town.

I clear my throat. "Fine, thanks," I answer, my words cardboard.

The man sneezes so hard that he nearly blows me across the store.

Lyon grabs a box of tissues and pushes them at Mr. Kryer. I step back, ready to dive for cover if his nose explodes again.

Lyon sticks the toothpick back between his lips and slides it to one side of his mouth. "You eat dinner? Dill made some fine chicken."

I scowl. If Lyon gives away the dinner that I'd made for *him*, I'll be spitting mad.

"I'm sure it's great." *Sniff.* "But I got to stop by a few more places, talk to some folks before I can head home to Mrs. Kryer's stew." Mr. Kryer pats what could be a watermelon under his plaid, button-down shirt. "That woman puts together a mean stew." He grins only a moment. "But I'm not here to talk about cooking. I'm here to spread the word about a big problem."

He sighs then. "This is the part I've been dreading." He looks at Lyon. "Tell me your dog has been home safe and sound."

"What? Sure, I guess." Lyon glances at me. "Dead End has been home, right, Dill?"

"I wouldn't bother you with this, knowing what your family has been through," Mr. Kryer puts in quick. "But we've got a problem with some dogs. A pack of them are running wild. They attacked one of Jim Wilson's sheep." *Sniff.* "Killed it. And well, someone thought he saw a yellow husky type, like your dog."

My heartbeat speeds up. I should have guessed that Mr. Kryer, our ex-mayor, would warn folks about the dogs. The man has a gift for getting people fired up over a cause. Every year, he organizes the county fair and the holiday toy drive for underprivileged kids, and manages to get folks excited about livestock and dolls.

"Sheriff Hawks is as angry as a wet hornet and has signed some of us up as assistant deputies to help him track down the bloodthirsty mutts and their irresponsible owners." Mr. Kryer puffs himself up, looking something like a rooster with a beer belly. "I'm bringing the farmers together for shooting lessons. I got Fred Barley, who's a real good shot, lined up to teach us a thing or two about hitting targets."

The thought of farmers shooting at dogs makes me gasp. But Lyon and Mr. Kryer ignore me as if I'm part of the woodwork.

"Sheriff Hawks has asked some of us to get the word out about the dogs." *Sniff.* Mr. Kryer pulls a page from his back pocket. "Can you hang this in your store, Lyon?"

"Of course." The page crinkles as he takes it, unfolds it, and then scans it.

I lean toward him, stretching my neck to see the writing. Bold, black, no-nonsense letters scream **WARNING!** ***Dog pack seen on Wilson farm. BLACK LABRADOR,*** ***GERMAN SHEPHERD, and BLOND HUSKY seen*** ***chasing sheep. Husky killed one sheep. Call Sheriff*** ***Hawks with any information.***

My heart beats hard enough to bust a rib. *Blond husky?* No wonder Mr. Kryer asked about Dead End. This page might as well be an F.B.I. ten most wanted list with Dead End's name on it. The whole town will see it if Lyon hangs the thing in his store.

Mr. Kryer grunts as he turns to the door, wiping his nose with the back of his hand again. "Hard enough making a living off of a farm these days without having to worry about people's pets attacking livestock."

Lyon's head bobs in agreement. He places Mr. Kryer's page on the counter, then follows the farmer to the door.

"You tell Hawks that I'll do anything I can to help," Lyon says as they move out to the parking lot. "Dogs that go after livestock should be destroyed."

That comment freezes me. I stand stunned until a truck door slams. And then, almost without thinking, I snatch Mr. Kryer's paper with shaking hands. I stuff it into my back pocket and head for the door.

"I got to get home," I tell Lyon as I hop onto my bike. "G.D.'s waiting."

Lyon's expression crinkles with questions, but I take off before he can say a word.

• • •

Clutching Mr. Kryer's warning, I drop the bag with the rawhide bone onto Dead End's dog bed, and then shoot across the ranch to my room.

Where can I hide the warning? I drop to my belly and peer under my bed. Dust balls remind me that I'm not keeping the ranch as eat-off-the-floor clean as Mom did.

My most valued treasures are *squirreled away,* as G.D. says, under this bed. The shoe box of my favorite letters and postcards from him, sent weekly from wher- ever he was. Lyon's good luck silver dollar, which he gave to me to put in my pocket during horse shows. Mom's overdue library books, which I still can't bring myself to return. The silver-handled hairbrush that she'd had since she was my age. And the last of her gardenia perfume.

Less important, but still under the bed, lays the stomach-medicine-pink diary with the matching pen, still in cellophane packaging. Lyon bought this stupid thing after Mrs. Doyle told him that I need to get my feelings out about Mom, one way or another. But there's no way I'm going to spill these in ink.

I push the diary aside and wrap my fingers around the small perfume bottle—my favorite treasure these days. After pulling it out, I carefully pop off the top, releasing the bone-deep comforting scent that sings Mom.

Mom. She'd be plenty disappointed in me for not telling Lyon about Dead End running off again, and for snatching Mr. Kryer's warning. My lies are bad enough. *You know better,* I can almost hear her say.

The door to the garage opens, and then closes. Lyon's boots stomp inside. "Dill?"

After replacing the top to the perfume bottle, I shove Mr. Kryer's page into my back pocket before heading for the kitchen. "Lyon! You're home!"

His big hands juggle overstuffed folders and the bagged dinner that I'd made. "Came by to finish the chicken with you and G.D.," he says over a toothpick. "Where is he?"

I look over my shoulder at his closed bedroom door. "Sleeping."

Lyon glances down at the brown bag. "Guess I am a little late." The toothpick slides to one side of his mouth as he looks at me. "By the way, did you see where I put that flyer Bob Kryer gave me?"

I shrug, wondering if this counts as another lie.

"I got to find it." Lyon turns away from me to dump the folders onto the counter. "A dog pack is bad news. Folks need to know about it."

This stabs. My insides clench.

Lyon drops his bagged dinner onto the counter. "Did you notice that the flyer said something about a blond husky in the pack?"

"Oh?" My voice squeaks.

"Where's Dead End?"

"Around somewhere," I manage to get out. "Sounds like that new dog up the road, the yellow husky-shepherd mix that is running with the dog pack." I'm not sure which feels worse, lying so easily, or knowing I'm half good at it.

"New dog?" Lyon pauses from flipping through papers, his back still turned.

"Yup," I say, thinking *you'd know the truth if you were home more.*

If Lyon wasn't all knotted up, he'd at least pick up on my shrugging and my clipped answers. He'd wonder about not having seen our dog. Lyon used to be the best at detecting my thoughts, moods, and actions. Mom called this his parent radar.

He pushes his fingers through his dark hair. "Fear of a dog pack will send the farmers to that new store for guns, traps, and poisons—all the things I don't carry at Mac-Gregor's." He scans the counter. "Dang. I forgot my receipts."

"The sheriff isn't going to let people use that stuff on dogs, is he?" My voice trembles.

Lyon lumbers back to the garage. "Out-of-control animals have to be stopped, Dill." The garage door slams shut behind him.

My hand goes to Mr. Kryer's flyer, which practically ticks like a time bomb in my pocket, reminding me that I'm not being fair to Lyon. The farmers will be more than mad if he doesn't hang this warning in his store. Other flyers are sure to be plastered like wallpaper all over town. Lyon could get more. He would, too. He cares that much about his friends and neighbors.

That's why I sidestep to the counter, and pull the paper from my pocket. As the garage door opens, I stuff the page into one of Lyon's folders, and then jump back from it.

"I got a bad feeling about these dogs," Lyon says as his boots stamp back into the kitchen, his hands gripping the folder of receipts.

"Me, too," I mutter.

CHAPTER 8

OLD AS DIRT

T HE SMELLS OF HORSE, HAY, AND GRAIN HANG IN the thick, stable air. Horses snort, shift, and stamp their hooves in nearby stalls. "You're late," I tell Cub. My hands itch to dump a pitchfork of dirty, stinking straw over his buzzed head.

Stepping into the box stall, he shifts on the untied laces of his work boots and plucks at his too-big, faded T-shirt. The Bayer family scent of bleach and fabric softener cling to his shirt and shorts, which are more wrinkled than used tissues. His mom shows her love for her family by the intense way that she does their laundry, but the woman hates ironing.

"We said we'd get the stable work done early this morning so we could go look for Dead End before my riding lesson. Remember?" Worrying about being late for my lesson makes me more cranky than usual and as tight as a pulled rubber band.

"Sorry," Cub says. "Timmy and Jimmy, the idiot twins, locked me in the basement." His face goes beet-purple as he stares at his work boots and kicks at hay pieces.

I dump old, wet straw into the wheelbarrow and stab the prongs of the pitchfork into more of it on the floor. "Okay, that rots, but we still need to find Dead End." I stop, don't say *before he goes after more animals* while listening for Skeeter, Jerry Smoothers, or anyone who might overhear me. "We got to find that dog before Sheriff Hawks does."

Socrates, one of Ms. Hunter's stable goats, clops up behind Cub and nuzzles his back pocket. When Cub doesn't pull out a garden carrot right away, Socrates plants the knobs of his would-be horns into Cub's butt and shoves him. Ms. Hunter has always said that she'd had both her goats dehorned for the safety of every rear end in the county.

"Nice hit, Socrates," I mumble.

Cub gives me a prune-faced look. "Who spit in your cornflakes this morning, Dill?" He pulls out a carrot. Socrates grabs it and trots off, probably sensing my mood.

I yank the fork from bedding. "G.D. is real down. He hasn't been eating. He didn't even go to the garden this morning."

Cub lets loose a sigh that weighs a ton. "Dill, I heard my mom on the phone with Mrs. Peterson this morning.

Dogs killed two of the Petersons' prize sheep last night."

The pitchfork handle slips from my hands, smacking the wall. "That's the second sheep attack this week."

"Both while Dead End has been gone." Now Cub kicks at straw.

"We got to get over there."

"Dill, those dogs are long gone by now and . . ."

I lift my hand in a stop signal because riding boots scuff the concrete outside the stall. "Listening in, again, Skeeter?"

He steps into the doorway, gripping his silver-handled crop. "What do you two know about the sheep killings?"

Cub whips around fast, almost dislocates his head from his neck. "Buzz off, Mosquito-breath."

"No, I won't *buzz off*," Skeeter whines. "The sheriff asked me to help him. I could turn you in."

As I step toward Skeeter, to wipe the know-it-all grin off his face, Ms. Hunter's riding boots smack the concrete fast, moving down an out-of-sight aisle. "Dill?" The tension in her voice echoes.

"Captain's stall," I call.

Ms. Hunter steps up behind Skeeter. She stands tall, as always, but her eyes are wide. Her mouth twitches.

She glances at Cub, then Skeeter before her blue-eyed

gaze settles on me. "Dill, your father called. We need to reschedule your riding lesson." She pushes past Skeeter and touches my shoulder in the same gentle way Mom used to do. My nose fills with the scents of saddle soap and horse. She blinks. "You need to get home."

My heart jerks, and suddenly feels as if someone has punched it. I shoot out of the stall.

"What's wrong?" Cub asks Ms. Hunter, the question echoing behind me.

"Dill's grandfather," Ms. Hunter tells him before I throw myself out of the stable and into the sun and heat.

The entire way home, as I pedal like some crazed maniac being chased by the devil himself, a thought tries to creep up from back in the crawl spaces of my mind: Could something being wrong with G.D. be a kind of punishment? Payback for my lies? Because somehow it makes sense that being good leads to rewards, while being anything less brings on trouble and heartache.

• • •

As my bike tires skid to a stop in our driveway, behind Doc Kerring's dusty and dented station wagon and Lyon's pickup truck, I almost stop breathing. It hasn't been long enough since I've seen Doc Kerring's old car on our property.

114

I shoot into the ranch, ripples of sweat skidding down the sides of my face.

"I hear that new store has an incredible computer system and data bank. And I hear it sells high-powered guns with scopes and all kinds of wild technical stuff," Doc Kerring says with too much enthusiasm. He sits with his broad back to me, leaning over our kitchen table—a sight I've seen too many times.

Lyon, slumped in his usual seat, holds his forehead in his hands. "Yup. That new store is something else. Farmers can even pick up gun permits there."

I stop short and stare at my riding boots because I can't look at Lyon for another second. I should let him know what's been going on with those farmers. I should tell him about Dead End. My hands go to the end of my ponytail, pull hard at it.

"Dill?"

When I look up, Lyon is staring at me. A toothpick droops between his lips. When I don't move, he stands; it takes him only two long strides to get to me.

"G.D.?" I barely squeeze this out, can't get out anymore.

Lyon's huge hands start to reach for my shoulders, but he stops himself, deciding to stay behind his wall. His hands drop to his sides. "G.D.'s resting. In bed."

At least he hasn't been taken to the hospital.

Doc Kerring, a walrus with a stethoscope, pushes himself up from his chair and turns to face me. He rubs the thick folds under his chin and presses his lips together, blinking a lot from behind his round, silver, wire-framed glasses—his serious, *we need to talk* look.

Lyon nudges me toward the kitchen, but I don't move.

Doc Kerring doesn't smile as he walks toward me. "Morning, Dill." He blinks again, clears his throat. He always does this before he delivers a shot, a pill, or bad news. "Dill, your granddad needs to go to the hospital for some tests."

I start backing away from the word *hospital,* shoot a glare at Lyon. How could he even think about sending his father there after what happened to Mom?

Pale as a peeled potato, Lyon's expression seems to plead with me. "Dill, the doctors will help G.D."

"Oh, yeah, the way they helped . . ." I stop short, still unable to say *Mom* out loud. I also don't ask, with sarcasm fueled by bubbling-hot anger, if the same hospital doctors will put poison into his blood and call it *treatment* the way they did with her.

Normally, Lyon would have a real problem with my sassy attitude, but now he seems to have no more energy than a bag of wood chips.

"Do I hear my girl?" G.D.'s voice trickles out from the guestroom that has become his bedroom.

I sprint across the kitchen and down the short hall to him.

Thick, warm shadows hang like ghosts in this room. The pulled-down shades hold in oily medicine smells. G.D. is on his back under a thin sheet. One of his bird-claw hands clutches the gold chain and rings, now outside his white T-shirt. The Civil War cane leans against the end of the bed as if waiting to be called into service again.

"Thought you had a riding lesson this morning, girl."

"You're more important than riding," I tell him, adding a wink because he knows there was a time when not a whole lot was more important to me than riding.

"Don't be giving up your lessons for me. They're about the only thing that gives you any kind of break from all the missing and the hurt."

I turn to the windows. "G.D.? Why are the shades down? You love sunshine." My voice wavers. My fake smile twitches. My hand goes to where his fragile hand rests on top of the sheet.

The pillow crinkles. The linen rustles as G.D. tries to push his old body up into a sitting position. "Old age is the devil's playground, Dill."

I sniff. "You'll be okay."

His fingers curl over mine in a weak, bony squeeze. "You know, even though the last nine months have been rougher than words can say, I've loved being with my only grandgirl. Makes me think I should have settled in with you folks earlier, the way you always asked me to."

I swallow hard, blinking fast, needing to refocus before the tears come. My eyes find a framed picture on the table beside G.D.'s bed: a black and white photograph of G.D.'s wife, Bets. Beside her, another frame holds a color picture of a puffed-up and proud, grinning Lyon holding a seven-year-old me on a pony. Mom had taken that picture. When she didn't have any more children, she'd tried to become a professional photographer. But she never took pictures of anyone or anything except Dead End and her animals, G.D., Lyon, and me.

"That photo shows when you and your pop were happy." G.D.'s voice comes out as dry and as cracked as old shoe leather.

That's when I notice the newest framed photo of Mom, clicked off the Christmas before she got sick. It's a fine picture of her snuggled up next to Lyon. He's turned away from the camera, but she's smiling into it, happy and healthy and ready to hop out of the silver frame. G.D. turns his head to stare into her eyes. This makes my throat close up. Quickly, I focus on a fourth frame.

118

This photo shows the warm eyes, yellow pointed ears, and panting enthusiasm of the cutest dog in the world. I can almost hear his thick tail thumping the kitchen floor. I can almost see him sitting beside Mom's bed, watching over her, licking her hand, whining and pacing around her bed as she moans in her restless sleep. Some images come this way, unwanted and un-invited.

If our dog was here now, he'd be fussing and staying close to G.D., too.

"That's a good picture of Dead End," I mutter, my voice trickling out.

G.D. lets go a heavy sigh, sounding like Lyon. "Changing the subject—every bit as bullheaded as your pop."

"Everything will be great." My voice splinters. *Everything will be great* belonged to Mom, and always brought comfort. But out of my mouth, it sounds empty. I quickly clear my throat. "G.D., can a dog be bad once in a while, but still be good overall?"

The pillowcase crinkles again as G.D. turns his face to me and squints. "What's on your mind, girl? What are you getting at?"

Since when has he lost his ability to see through me? Like Lyon, G.D. has always known me better than I know myself. Not willing to share my itching doubts about Dead End, I shrug, stiff and uncomfortable in my own skin. "I've been thinking about those pack dogs. That's all."

G.D. grunts and turns his head away from me. "You're worried about Dead End. You're wondering if he could be part of the pack." G.D. sucks in a long breath. "Me, too. Wish I could get him to that shelter in Utah. That might be the only way to save the dog's hide. But I can't get anywhere now."

G. D.'s free hand moves across the sheet, toward me. I drop my free hand to his twig bones and tissue-paper skin. "Lyon and that doctor want me to go to the hospital," G.D. says in a low and weary voice. He turns his face back to me, his sky-blue eyes moist. "Think I might go."

A volt of fear rips through me and rattles my bones. "No! You can't. You won't come back." I turn away from him and focus on his old trunk at the back of the room, trying to stay calm, trying not to remember.

The trunk holds his wandering souvenirs: the floppy hat from the South Carolina sailor, a blanket from New Mexico, and a handmade, turquoise-decorated dog collar that G.D. puts on Dead End during special occasions, like July 8th, the day G.D. brought the pooch to us; the day we always celebrated, complete with Mom's chocolate cake, as Dead End's birthday. My free hand goes to the pocket that holds the picture of Mom and Lyon. "You promised me that you wouldn't go to any hospital, ever."

"Dill." Lyon's commanding voice bounces off the doorway. "Dr. Kerring says G.D. needs to go to the hospital. This is different than when your mother . . ."

"Lyon." G.D.'s voice, weak but firm, interrupts. "I've changed my mind. I'm not going after all."

"But Pop, we agreed. . . ."

"Changed my mind, son."

Lyon looks at me, his eyes wide and startled. Then he looks back at G.D. "But the hospital's the best place for you right now, Pop. Dr. Kerring said . . ."

"Made up my mind," G.D. repeats, interrupting.

Lyon's lips go tight over the toothpick, nearly snapping the thing in two. "Dill," he says, turning his face to me. "You can't let your fear keep G.D. from getting the care he needs."

Doc Kerring adjusts his silver-framed glasses as he comes up behind Lyon. "Mr. MacGregor, the hospital . . ."

"No." G.D.'s hand lifts from mine and then thumps onto the sheets. The birds outside seem to stop chattering. "I don't need a test to tell me that I'm as old as dirt. No one can stick a tube in my arm and give me back thirty years."

Lyon sighs, and steps up behind me. "Okay, Pop. Get some sleep." His big, firm hand comes down onto my shoulder, and then guides me to the doorway.

When I glance back at G.D., he winks.

"Everything will be great," I mutter to him. But first, I have to find Dead End. I have to get that dog home.

CHAPTER 9 BLACKIE

"Hey." My tone is dull, heavy. Stepping into the grain room, I wipe at my damp forehead. Even though my riding lesson ended twenty minutes ago, I'm still as limp and as wet as a used washrag. The day's heat is already sticking to me like new flypaper.

"Morning, Dill." Cub looks up, slightly squinting at me the way he does when trying to read my mood.

"Sorry I'm late. Even though I didn't get here on time, Ms. Hunter let me ride the full hour." Horses crunch grain and snort. The sweet scents of molasses, corn, and oats mix with my favorite stable smells of hay and saddle leather. "Guess I missed feeding the horses this morning."

Grain spatters into a steel garbage can. "No big deal." Cub lowers the bag of feed and looks smack at me. "Has Dead End come home?"

Focusing on the toes of my dusty riding boots now, I shake my head. "No."

Cub grunts. "I was hopin' you were late because he'd shown up."

"No. I was late because G.D. wanted to talk more about how I need to face life head-on." I grind my boot heel into a corn kernel, mashing it, sick of hearing about what I should and shouldn't do. "He keeps trying to get me to go with Lyon to . . ." I hesitate. "You know."

"Fairfax." Cub goes to one of the traps that Jerry Smoothers keeps placing around the stable, trying to cut down the mouse and rat populations. With a kick, Cub springs the trap, making its jaws bite closed so that it becomes harmless. I swear the kid would sacrifice a toe to keep even a mangy rat from getting a whisker caught in a trap. "How's G.D.?"

"He slept right through our usual breakfast time. Another reason I'm late."

Cub makes a grunting sound which might as well say *that's not good*. He knows G.D. usually gets up before the rooster crows.

I suck in a breath. Even during my lesson, I couldn't shake the image of G.D., looking too brittle, making his way from his bedroom to the kitchen. "He'll be fine once Dead End comes home." My voice, like my insides, trembles.

Cub raises his eyebrows, showing his doubt.

"Once Dead End comes home, everything will be

great," I say again, barely getting this out, trying to believe it. But even Mom's words sound weak today.

"What if Dead End doesn't come back?"

"I've told you—he *will*," I snap. "He's a good dog. Sad, but still good."

Cub kicks another trap shut. "Dill, maybe the dog bein' missing isn't what's bothering your grandfather. Maybe G.D. really does need to go to the hospital."

I shake my head hard because I don't have any more words to argue with.

Cub flips over the now-useless trap with his boot toe. "And that's why Donny has started calling you Cleopatra, Queen of Denial."

"What?"

"Yeah. Because you never come over anymore and won't talk to my dad about what's happened. Because you won't deal with . . ." Cub stops. "Well, you know."

I don't breathe. Donny talking about me? Cleopatra sounds great, but *Queen of Denial*? Calling me *Queen Freak* would sound better.

"Get it?" Cub grins. "Denial sounds like Nile. Cleopatra was the queen of the Nile."

"Yeah, I get it," I bark.

Before I can get all over Cub about whatever else Donny might have said about me, the sound of boots coming fast down the aisle stops me. Ms. Hunter pauses in the grain room doorway, her eyes wide with alarm, the fingers of her right hand wrapped around her small cell phone. "Dill, Cub. Have you seen Dr. Kitt?"

Cub jerks his thumb left. "Black Bart's stall."

Ms. Hunter whips around, her long red braid flying. The frantic thud of her riding boots echoes through the stable.

"Come on," I say low to Cub, waving at him to follow me.

At the end of the aisle, I stop, and stick my arm out to stop Cub from shooting past me. As we peer around a corner, Ms. Hunter jogs past two stalls and then slows at Black Bart's space.

"Give us a look at that leg, Bart," Dr. Kitt says in his raspy, sandpaper voice. He always refers to himself as *us* or *we* when he speaks to his animal patients.

Ms. Hunter grabs either side of the doorway of Black Bart's stall as if she needs to hold herself up. "Ian, Ned Jonas shot a dog. About ten minutes ago."

I gasp, slapping a hand over my mouth. Cub makes a sound like he's about to lose his breakfast.

"*Shot a dog?*" Dr. Kitt's question comes out breathless. "Ned Jonas wouldn't swat a fly if it bit him."

I grab Cub's arm and yank him into an empty box stall.

"Your wife called a few minutes ago." Ms. Hunter lifts her cell phone. "Ned Jonas got ahold of her. She said he sounded frantic. Something about dogs chasing his sheep. He shot at them. *Hit one!*"

"Ned doesn't even own a gun."

"Apparently, he does now," Ms. Hunter adds, her voice dropping.

Cub jabs me in the ribs with his elbow—his own weapon. "Old Mr. Jonas probably got that gun from the new store," he spits in a whisper.

All at once I feel like I've swallowed a gallon of milk gone sour.

Metal clinks—has to be Dr. Kitt throwing his veterinarian tools into his bag. "Something has to be done about that dog pack before every farmer in the county starts shooting at anything that moves."

Cub gulps. "What if . . . ?"

A zipper rips—probably on Dr. Kitt's medical bag—interrupting Cub. "Tucker, could you call my wife?" The man sounds tense. "Tell her I'm on my way to Ned's place."

I grab Cub's arm. "We'll go to the Jonas's farm, too," I whisper, my voice shaking.

The quick beat of Ms. Hunter's riding boots comes back at us. "Ned told your wife that he'd be at his barn with the dog, waiting for you."

"I'm as good as there." Dr. Kitt's steps follow her.

As they pass us, Cub and I drop and press against the stall wall to keep from being seen. When the footsteps fade, I straighten. "If we cut through Drake's Farm on our bikes," I whisper, "we could get to the Jonas place almost as quick as Dr. Kitt."

Cub gives me one of those big grins that announce he's up for anything. "Sounds like one of your plans, Dill." His eyes almost twinkle. "I've missed those."

"Aren't there a couple sheds sort of near the Jonas barn?"

"Yeah." Cub's face twists as he considers this. "We might be able to sneak into one without being seen, but we'll have to be real careful about it."

"Good enough," I say. "Let's go."

• • •

"The tractor shed is the safest building to get into," Cub tells me as he herds me through the tall stalks of a cornfield behind the Jonas barn. "I'm not sure what we'll see from there, but if we try to get into any of the other buildings, we'll be spotted for sure." With that, he leads me into a three-sided, shadowy plank shack close to the corn.

My heart punches a rib-busting rhythm to the beat of *Dead End couldn't have been shot, Dead End couldn't have been shot.* My quivering fingers wipe sweat droplets from my forehead. What will I tell G.D. if something bad has happened to our dog? The man can't take much more loss. None of us can.

"I discovered this shed last summer, when Danny and Tommy made me help them bale hay for old Mr. Jonas." Cub squeezes past ancient and oily tractors, plows, and wagons—metal dinosaurs that smell of gasoline, corn, and hay. "I'd sneak off and hide in here to get a break," he whispers. "They never could find me."

I scrape past a tractor tire. "How are we going to see anything from in here?"

Cub jerks his thumb at the gaps between the warped planks.

Once we get to the back wall, I squint into a space almost as wide as my hand. "Cub," I breathe, "I see Dr. Kitt." It's hard to miss his floppy green-and-blue plaid hat. Short and stocky, he's kneeling over something laid out in front of the huge barn—a stone's throw from Cub and me. Wiry Mr. Jonas stands close by Dr. Kitt. The three grown Jonas boys hover beside him, towering over their dad. Given Dr. Kitt's back, Mr. Ned Jonas's back, and the tree-trunk legs of the Jonas sons, Cub and I can't see even the fur of the flat-out patient.

"I got a bad feelin'," Cub mutters.

My stomach hiccups, but a distant metallic rumble, growing louder by the second, stops me from agreeing with him.

"A truck." Cub throws himself over plows and bounces off a tractor tire, scrambling to a gap in the side wall. "A blue pickup tearin' down the driveway," he reports. "Mr. Crowley's truck."

I groan. "That hothead has a habit of causing tons of trouble." Even Lyon, who gets along with everybody, had a run-in with Mr. Pete Crowley once. "Remember when Mr. Crowley went berserk because Lyon wouldn't let Blackie wander around the store off her leash?"

Cub rolls his eyes. "Yup," he says as the truck skids to a stop, spraying dirt and gravel that pelts our shed like bullets. "Jeez." He backs away from the wall. "Mr. Crowley looks as mad as a wet cat."

As I wipe at my eyes and spit dust, Cub throws himself back at the wall facing the barn, almost cracking his leg bone on a plow.

The truck door whips open. "Ned! What's going on?" Mr. Crowley's voice explodes like a cannon.

I find a gap, peer out at hairy-armed Mr. Crowley— a grizzly bear in denim and suspenders. He stands scowling with his big hands on his hips, poised for battle. The knot of men in front of Cub and me shift and turn to stare at him.

It doesn't matter that I'd pass out if I saw yellow fur, I still shift and dip, trying to see past all the legs and sagging denim butts. Mom always warned me that curiosity could kill cats. This had never stopped me before, but now something tells me that I should hang on to her words.

Mr. Pete Crowley storms toward the group. "Ned, why'd your wife call me over here?"

Dr. Kitt straightens and turns, giving Cub and me a glimpse of half of his face, enough to reveal a sadness that hangs on him like a bag of wet sand. The wall of bodies breaks apart around what has to be the shot dog as Mr. Jonas and his boys step back.

"Blackie." Cub's elbow slams into my already bruised ribs.

"Not Dead End." There could be no better medicine for G.D.

But Mr. Crowley jerks back. All color leaves his face. "Blackie?" For once, his voice doesn't thunder. He blinks as if he doesn't believe his eyes.

Dr. Kitt sighs. "I'm sorry, Pete. I did what I could."

My breath lumps in my throat. My heart suddenly feels like it's on the prongs of a pitchfork.

Cub jerks back from the wall as if it has bitten him. "Mr. Jonas shot Blackie?"

All relief and joy from knowing Dead End hasn't been hurt evaporates. Blackie, the playful Labrador with a tail that never stopped. A smiling sweetheart of a dog. The mother of the pup Cub's parents wouldn't let him keep.

"I just took care of her a couple weekends ago," Cub mutters, his tone disbelieving. "Brought her a new tennis ball."

Images like photographs pop into my head: Blackie barely able to sit still, her brown eyes bright and anxious as she waits for Cub to throw a ball; Blackie paddling across the Crowley's pond to retrieve a stick; Blackie smiling, proud of the four adorable, fat and wriggling pups around her.

Cub turns away from me, sniffs, wipes at his eyes.

With clenched fists, Mr. Crowley turns on Mr. Jonas. "What'd you do to my dog?"

Mr. Ned Jonas points a gnarled finger back at Mr. Crowley. "She went after my sheep. You should have kept her on your own property."

Mr. Crowley's face goes crimson. I'd have bet my stable pay that he'd squash Mr. Jonas like a bug, but Dr. Kitt pushes between them, his hands up in stop signals. "You two don't need to make this situation any worse."

Another engine rumble interrupts. Within a minute, gravel and dirt spray the driveway side of the shed again. Everyone turns to the black-and-white sheriff's car as it slides to a stop near Mr. Crowley's truck.

Cub sniffs again, and then slides the back of his hand under his nose.

The driver's side door of the patrol car flies open. Sheriff Tom Hawks jumps out from behind the steering wheel, reminding me of a Doberman pinscher guard dog. As he yanks his mirrored sunglasses off his face, his dark eyes narrow on Mr. Crowley. "What's going on here?"

Cub presses his face to the gap. If he doesn't become a vet, he'll be a sheriff.

Dr. Kitt tips his head at Mr. Jonas and Mr. Crowley. "Ned here shot Pete's Blackie, Tom."

"Because that Blackie and some other dogs went after my sheep!"

Sheriff Hawks growls something about stinkin' dog packs, and then points at Mr. Jonas. "Got a license for the gun, Ned?"

"Yup. Got it the other day from that new store in Blacksberry."

Cub moans low in his throat, sounding like he might hurl.

Mr. Crowley waves a tight fist. "I don't care if Santa Claus brought him the damn gun! He shot my dog!"

"I might have clipped another in the pack, too," Mr. Jonas mutters. "Can't be sure."

The sheriff turns to Blackie, stares at her, his eyes heavy with a sadness I don't expect. More than once,

Mom and Lyon have used this man as an example of the tough, no-nonsense type who practices patience and fairness. Whenever I lose my temper, like the time I'd called Jeanie Snipes a low-life tramp, even though I hadn't a clue what that meant, Lyon reminds me of the fair and generous ways of Sheriff Hawks.

"Any witnesses?" The sheriff kneads his forehead.

"The missus and Ida Gilford," Mr. Jonas says, exhaustion weighing on his tone. "They were havin' coffee in the kitchen when they looked out the window and saw dogs take after my sheep."

"I'll have to speak with those ladies." The sheriff takes a deep breath and turns to Dr. Kitt. "Cause of death?"

Death stabs my ears, pierces through my center as if I'm made of butter.

"Bullet wounds," Dr. Kitt states.

Mr. Crowley drops his face into his hands and turns away from everyone. A strangled noise escapes from Cub.

The image of Dead End smiling pushes into my head. Suffocating sadness wraps around me, and squeezes the air out of my lungs.

"Poor Blackie," Cub whispers.

Sheriff Hawks pulls out a pad of paper and a pen. "What a mess," he says while scribbling. "I'm sorry about Blackie, Pete, but Ned had a license. I'll check out his statements, but it seems Blackie was part of that dog pack we've been dealing with."

Mr. Crowley stiffens. His top lip curls up in a snarl. The guard dogs at Rusty's junkyard look less vicious. "Blackie's never gone after sheep."

"Pete," Dr. Kitt says. "We all know Blackie was a fine dog—a good pet."

Another strangled noise escapes from Cub.

The sadness I've been struggling to keep down bubbles up into my chest. My bottom lip begins to quiver and my eyes fill. An urge to run back to the stable, jump onto Crossfire's back and ride hard and long, gallop away from this mess, even if that means leaving Virginia itself, almost takes me over.

"A Labrador retriever isn't a killer," Mr. Crowley says. "Especially not Blackie."

He sounds like me defending Dead End.

Dr. Kitt sighs. "Often, when a dog experiences pack hunting and the thrill of chasing animals . . . when a dog tastes blood . . ." He scans the group before he looks back at Mr. Crowley. "It can't stop killing. Instinct takes over."

Again Cub jabs me. "Like Dead End and that poor groundhog."

I'm too busy fighting back a sob to speak.

Sheriff Hawks slides his sunglasses back onto his

face. "I've seen dogs come together in a pack before and it's not pretty. I'm sorry, Pete."

Dr. Kitt nods.

Cub covers his face with his hands and turns away from me.

Mr. Crowley drops to Blackie, lifts her body, and stomps back to his truck. "This dog pack business is a load of crap!" He lowers Blackie into the truck bed as if she is sleeping and he doesn't want to wake her. Standing there a minute, staring down at her, he wipes a hand over his face. Then he throws himself behind the steering wheel of his truck and slams the door closed.

"It's tough to accept," Dr. Kitt says as the blue truck tears back down the driveway.

Sheriff Hawks stuffs his writing pad and pen back into his pocket. "But unfortunately, the only way to stop a dog pack is to get rid of all the animals in it." He sucks in a deep breath. "And it's my job to make sure that happens."

I step back as if slapped. Lyon's voice explodes in my ears: *Dogs that go after livestock should be destroyed.*

CHAPTER 10 # CAUGHT

Only twenty-four hours later, Blackie's death hangs over me, too close to another loss only three months old and a missing pooch with golden eyelashes. Even being on Crossfire's back isn't pushing all other thoughts aside. I've lost what Ms. Hunter calls my *edge*, and almost fell off twice already during the last hour of my lesson. Instead of concentrating on trotting and cantering and jumping, I keep going back to sitting with G.D. at breakfast, trying to tell him about Blackie, but only listening to him talk about the importance of facing troubles head-on.

"Did you hear the good news, Dill?" Ms. Hunter crosses the center of the ring now that Crossfire and I are walking, cooling down. "Bob Kryer thinks he and his son caught one of the pack dogs. A blond husky."

I almost fall off Crossfire again. "Oh? Really?" My voice seeps out high-pitched and strangled. Thank goodness Ms. Hunter doesn't know all the dogs around here, and may not realize that Dead End is as yellow as corn.

For once, I'm glad she doesn't allow dogs in her stable, a precaution to keep her goats and the barn cats safe.

"Apparently, Bob lured this dog into the barn with Mrs. Kryer's stew." Ms. Hunter chuckles at this.

I picture Mom serving Dead End some of *her* famous stew, one of his favorite meals. Whenever he gulped it down, he'd give her happy dog grunts and wag his tail in big O's. Afterwards, he'd lick Mom's face in thanks, which she never turned away from, even though he had beef-gravy breath.

Ms. Hunter gets more serious as she focuses on me again. "Hey, sit up straight, Dill. Shoulders back. Walking Crossfire out doesn't mean you can ride like a rag doll."

I suck in air and squeeze my shoulder blades together, wishing I could shake off the image of Blackie lying like roadkill on the driveway of the Jonas farm.

"What's Mr. Kryer going to do with that dog?" My voice wobbles as my mind pictures G.D., his grin covering his face like paint, smothering Dead End with pets.

Ms. Hunter sighs as she heads toward the gate. "Put it to sleep."

No. Please, no!

"Let's call it quits for today, Dill. Your mind isn't on riding."

"Sorry," I manage to get out, hoping she doesn't connect my off day with my recent lack of enthusiasm for training and showing. I don't want her to know that I've been losing the love, the energy for competition. Would she still let me ride Crossfire if my heart wasn't in it?

She glances over her shoulder, throwing me a reassuring smile. "We all have off days. Crossfire still got a good workout, even if you didn't." But when she pauses at the gate, her smile evaporates. "But, Dill?" She focuses on my eyes, and hesitates as if wrestling with what she wants to tell me, which isn't her natural way. "Are you okay? Is there anything you want to share with me? I worry about you. I'm concerned with how you are coping with . . ."

"I'm great," I say, quick enough to cut her off and loud enough for the entire stable to hear. "Just thinking about how to best take that combination of jumps we've been working on," I add, even though I know what she's really asking about.

Ms. Hunter keeps studying me. "Dill, I'm talking about how you're coping with . . ."

"Everything is fine," I snap. And then I force a quick smile, hoping Ms. Hunter doesn't hear the bite in my words.

"Okay. But know that I'm here if you ever need me." She heads back to the barn. "You know the rules.

Walk Crossfire out before you put him back into his stall."

But I've got to find Cub fast, I want to scream. Has he heard that Mr. Kryer has trapped a yellow dog? I let the reins slide through my fingers as Ms. Hunter disappears into the stable. But instead of relaxing, Crossfire tenses. He pricks his ears and turns his head toward the woods.

I run my hand over his neck, head to shoulders. "What do you hear?" I whisper, not taking his reaction too seriously. This horse spooks easy, always has. "You hear another horse?" But no horses are out on the trails this hot summer afternoon.

Crossfire turns one ear back to my voice, but only for a second before leaves rustle near the path leading into the woods. Twigs snap.

Saddle leather creaks as I swing my leg over Crossfire's back and slide to a soft thud, landing on my feet. Clutching the reins, I lead Crossfire out the gate opening. But when I turn to go to the woods, he stiffens, throws his head up, showing the whites of his eyes, refusing to move in that direction. "Okay, okay," I tell him in my most soothing voice. Then I lead him back to the barn, even though my heart is thumping *Get to those trees! Get to those trees!*

Inside the stable, Crossfire's hooves clip-clop quicker than they should because I can hardly stop myself from breaking into a run.

"Who set your jeans on fire, Dill?" Cub, sitting on stacked straw bales outside Crossfire's stall, spits crumbs, his cheeks bulging with one of the peach muffins that I baked this morning. His shoulders are slouched. Misery with Blackie's name on it pulls on his face. "Better be careful. You know Mr. Smoothers lives to catch people breaking stable rules."

"Don't take another bite of that muffin!" I about jump on Cub. Crossfire jerks his head up again, startled.

Cub turns the half-eaten muffin up and over, studying it. "Looks all right to me."

"There's something in the woods, near the path—an animal. Maybe it's—" My voice cracks through my strained whisper. "Save the muffin to give to him."

"Whatever you heard out there, it's not Dead End, Dill." Cub's face tips down as he shakes his head slow. "I've been waiting here tryin' to figure out the best way to tell you that Mr. Kryer caught a dog. A blond husky mix."

"Yeah, I heard. But that dog isn't our dog."

"There you go being the Queen of Denial again."

"He loves my baking. We'll use that muffin you're chewing on to lure him out from the trees." I barely get this out before Crossfire pulls me into his stall. I unbuckle the girth, and haul the saddle off his back.

Cub comes to the doorway. "Dill, you need to face facts. Mr. Kryer has got your dog. I know your granddad is sick, but you got to tell him. He'd want to know."

I about throw the saddle, and then my helmet, at him. "Dead End is out there." I point in the general direction of the woods. "I know it." I unfasten the bridle so fast that my fingers almost tangle. Then I fling the thing onto a straw bale even though putting equipment away and brushing down a horse after riding are strict stable requirements. "He loves people. It makes sense that he'd come here. Let's go. We got to get him back to the ranch, keep him inside until the killings stop and . . ."

"Hush, Dill!" Cub waves his hands to shush me, almost flinging the remains of the muffin at my head. "Skeeter is here with his mother. Haven't you heard them? She's been shakin' the walls with all her bellowin'. And he's been hollerin' at poor Miss Velvet." Cub twists his head to one side and spits the way his brothers do when they're disgusted, as long as their mother isn't around. "Makes me sick the way he treats his horse." He spits again. If he keeps at this spewing, he'll dry up for sure.

"Forget about Skeeter and come with me." I head back toward the barn door. "And bring what's left of that muffin."

• • •

When we get close to the trail in the woods behind the barn, leaves crackle and twigs snap. Something deep enough into the trees to keep us from seeing it swishes under brush and dried-out leaves. I picture Dead End's windshield-wiper tail sweeping the ground.

"It's Dead End. I know it." I have to stop myself from jumping up and down and screaming with more joy than I've felt in months.

"Dill, there's nothin' but squirrels in there."

"Squirrels? Yeah, maybe if they're fifty pounds each," I snap.

Cub rolls his eyes, scratches his buzzed head, and grunts in a way that sounds like frustration. "If that's Dead End in there, then what dog did Mr. Kryer trap?"

I don't bother saying *who cares*. I start toward the trees, at least until Cub stops me by grabbing my arm as if my staying put is a matter of life or death. "Hold up." He drops into a squat, squinting and leaning toward the scrappy brambles. "If your dog is in there and he's not coming out to us, there's a reason why."

"Of course there's a reason," I spit, getting plenty impatient. "He feels bad for killing that groundhog and then running off. He knows that was wrong."

Cub inches closer to the trees. "Yeah well, if he's feelin' that guilty, we've got to be real gentle with him or he'll bolt again." Cub opens his hand, pushes his open palm with the mashed muffin on it toward the shadowy woods. "Is that you, boy? Come on out, let Dill and I see you. We miss you, even if you do have groundhog breath."

"Get closer," I whisper. "See if you can get an eyeful of him."

"Remember, he's got no collar to grab hold of."

I hold my breath and watch Cub push the mangled muffin into the shadows.

"Come here, Dead End. Come on, good dog," I say in my sweetest coaxing tone, even though my insides are tense enough to snap.

Cub extends his arm as far as he can. "If we had a groundhog sandwich," he grunts, "we could get that dog to come to us from anywhere."

If we hadn't been occupied, I'd have clobbered Cub for that.

But then leaves and twigs crackle and crunch as whatever is in the woods moves away from us.

"Cub," I squeak, "do something. He's getting away."

"Squirrels," Cub mutters again. But then he sighs. "If Dead End is here, maybe it's best to let him go." He sounds too calm, like his minister father when the man offers up advice you don't want but need to take, like foul-tasting medicine. "Plato and Socrates are outside. Dead End could go after them."

I jerk as if Cub has slapped me, then stand, and plant my hands hard on my hips. "Have you been sniffing the hoof dressing? How could you say something that ugly about my dog?" About Mom's dog.

"Dill," Cub says in that steel-hard way that announces he's about had enough. "I know you don't want to hear this, but it's about time you face facts." He stares right into my eyes then, giving me his *I will have my say* look.

I know better than to mess with him when he gets like this.

"You're too busy forcing things to be the way you want them to be to see what's real. You need to accept Dead End for the dog he is, not the dog you want him to be."

"He *is* a good dog," I squeak, my gusto gone. I don't sound even close to convinced anymore.

"Donny's right," Cub adds. "You are the Queen of Denial."

I turn and stomp off, too tired to fight about this.

"You've got the only husky dog around," Cub keeps on, coming after me. "If you really believe he's innocent, why do you keep throwing out lies?"

I don't answer, can't answer as we move along the side of the barn.

"How can you not even consider the possibility of your dog being a sheep killer when all the evidence is there, bold as red paint on a white wall?"

"A-ha!" Skeeter leaps out at us from a side entrance, waving his stupid, silver-handled crop like he is going to chop off our heads with it. "CAUGHT you! Knew I would! I knew you had something to do with the dog pack. Knew it!" Skeeter stabs the tip of his crop into my shoulder.

I smack the whip away. "You haven't *caught* us at anything, *Skeeter*."

"Oh yes, I have." He grins big, gloating. "The dog Mr. Kryer caught is your dog, isn't it, Dill?"

"No, it's not, Skeeter," Cub says, puffing himself, defending me in a shaky way that isn't the usual, confident Cub. "That dog Bob Kryer has got is a new dog in town—a big, yellow cuss of a mutt. Dill's dog has been at her house during all the sheep killings."

Skeeter's eyes shrink. "Don't give me that. I heard you call Dill's dog a sheep killer."

Words don't come to me. My heart beats a panicked *Say something! Say something!* Cub looks stunned, cornered and red-faced.

Skeeter almost glows with his triumph. The Mosquito. "Wait until Ms. Hunter and Sheriff Hawks hear this." The thin crease of Skeeter's mouth curls up at the corners in the ugliest grin I've ever seen. "No more free riding lessons for Dill." He spits out my name as if it's moldy cheese in his mouth. "No more being Ms. Hunter's favorite because she feels sorry for you. Because your mother . . ."

With my fists clenched, I lunge at him before he can finish. "You sack of . . ."

"Dill! No!" Cub grabs my arm, holds me back.

"You both have to treat me better now," Skeeter says. "You have to include me in whatever you're up to. We'll hang out. Because only the best of pals keep their secrets from other people, right?"

"Pal around with you? After all the cra—" Cub stops himself. "After all the *stuff* you've put us through?" Cub's grip strangles my arm. "That'll be the day, *Skeeter*," he practically hisses, as slow and as mean as Cub can get.

Skeeter's grin disappears. "Miss Velvet needs her stall mucked out."

"Then go muck," I snap, still itching to pound him for what he almost said.

"No, beef-brain. *You're* going to do it." Skeeter pokes the crop tip at me again. "Cub cleans out stalls for you. That's why you'll shovel out my horse's stall for me. Because that's what friends do for each other and I want people to see that we're *friends* now."

Cub narrows his eyes at Skeeter. "There'll be snow-skiing in hell before that happens."

Cub's curse floors me, cools my fury. I stand stunned. It was bad enough that he almost said *crap*. Even *thinking* a swear word gets a Bayer boy's mouth washed out with the slimy side of a soap bar.

Skeeter points the crop at Cub, then me. "Muck out Miss Velvet's stall or I'll tell Ms. Hunter, Sheriff Hawks, and anyone who'll listen about you owning a sheep-killing dog."

Every inch of my body wants to pound Skeeter senseless. But if I even breathe on him, he'll open his big mouth, and tell Ms. Hunter and Sheriff Hawks about Dead End. Everything Skeeter has seen and heard will get back to Lyon. And G.D.

"Fine. I'll deal with your stupid stall," I snarl. "And then I'll take the manure and shove it . . ."

"Dill!" Cub shoots me a warning look.

"Also, tell Ms. Hunter that you're withdrawing from the regional show." Skeeter's malicious grin snakes across his face again.

148

"What?" I can't have heard him right.

"You're pushing your stinkin' luck," Cub tells Skeeter.

He lifts his chin, throws his shoulders back, full of himself. "Sheriff Hawks asked me to help track down the pack dogs. I could remind him that you have a husky-type dog, Dill. I could tell him how that dog has been missing. How Cub talked about you lying." Skeeter struts back into the stable. "Withdraw from that horse show, Dill, or I *will* tell him. I'll turn your mutt in."

When he giggles, I lunge at him. Luckily, Cub grabs my arm again and points inside the barn where Stubs, low to the ground, begins stalking Skeeter. Any minute, the big barn cat will pounce and send him into a spinning fit.

"We'd better get out of here," Cub says, sounding more down and out than I've ever heard him. "Before one of us does something to that Mosquito that will get us into even deeper trouble than we're already in."

CHAPTER 11

ATTACKED

THE NEXT MORNING, CUB FINDS ME IN THE KITCHEN, measuring flour, sugar, and blueberries using Mom's dented and scratched metal measuring cups. As I dump the ingredients into the ceramic bowls that she's had since forever, I think again about how using her cooking stuff brings her back into the kitchen. Sort of. But not enough, not the way I need her to be—within reach and listening, helping me work out my problems.

"Do you think Ms. Hunter will be mad if I withdraw from the horse show?" My voice sounds whinier than a cat caught in cold rain. And I hate whiny.

Cub shakes his head. This doesn't surprise me, really. Sometimes I think he knows, has known for a while, that I could use a break from competing.

He picks up Mom's favorite wooden mixing spoon. He studies the handle, dotted with tiny dents from my baby teeth. He's held this spoon a thousand times, but right now it fascinates him. He blinks at it with faraway eyes that tell me he's thinking about Mom, probably missing her cooking, probably remembering how she always gave him this spoon covered in sweet batter, to lick clean. She always did a little extra for Cub, gave him more attention than my other friends, knowing he didn't get many treats like batter spoons in his household of eight. I swear this brought Cub over here more. The boy soaked up her attention the way a sun-baked field absorbs a summer rain.

After a long moment, Cub focuses on me again. "How are we gonna act like the Mosquito is our friend?" He sounds defeated, as if climbing the Blue Ridge Mountains in an hour would be easier than being nice to Skeeter.

"He's got no proof about our dog," I say. I take the wooden spoon from Cub and start stirring the batter.

Cub rolls his eyes, all impatient. "He does if Bob Kryer has Dead End."

"Which he doesn't," I state as plain as possible. "We saw the pooch yesterday. In the woods."

"I didn't see any dog, Dill."

I stop stirring and stare at him for a long minute. "What's got you all bitter and sour?"

He glares at me then. "I lied, Dill. I jumped right in, spit out your lie about that new yellow dog to Skeeter." Cub looks down, shakes his head. "And I said *h-e* double hockey sticks."

"Skeeter could make anyone curse. He . . ."

"I don't want him makin' me do anything," Cub yells. And then he waves me away. "Ah, never mind. You don't get it."

I scoop batter into the compartments of Mom's muffin tin, giving Cub a minute, knowing not to mess with him when he gets like this. I don't even bother explaining that I *do* get what is bugging him. Neither of us can take being forced to do anything, and especially not by Skeeter. "Okay," I say as I slide the baking tray into the oven. "Come on. Let's go check on G.D. while breakfast bakes."

• • •

As we step through the back doorway and into the yard, Cub points at the garden.

"G.D.," I call, happy.

He turns our way, offers a struggling smile while leaning on the picket fence that surrounds the neat rows of bold orange marigolds that alternate between strips of cucumbers, broccoli, lettuce, and tomatoes. "Your mama swore that those flowers, the pumpkin-colored ones, would keep the bugs and critters away from the vegetables," he says as we get to him. "She was right." He shakes his head. "Such a smart woman."

My throat closes up and my chest swells from listening to him talk about Mom with a longing and sadness I understand too well.

"Got a call from Bob Kryer."

I freeze. Cub groans, pulls on his hair, shoots me an *I told you so* look.

G.D. keeps staring at the vegetables. "Bob is pretty sure he's caught one of the pack dogs." G.D. turns to look at me then, the wrinkles crevice-deep around his frown, a glassy glaze over his eyes. "A yellow husky mix with a split ear. Sounds like our dog, girl." The focus of his gaze drops to his boots. "Bob admitted that he's had suspicions about our pooch being a part of the pack, but he didn't want to say anything until he was certain."

I stare at my granddad without moving. The world keeps spinning, but without me. "That dog can't be Dead End," I say. But my argument has little fight left in it.

"Dill, the dog Bob caught has a shoulder wound, as if he'd been grazed by a bullet." G.D.'s hand grips his cane harder. "Ned Jonas shot at dogs when they chased his sheep."

I start to argue that this means squat, until hooves thud across Mr. Barley's field, a piece of land that stretches out to our left, along the side of our property.

Two young steer bolt through an opening in a bramble hedge that separates the field into sections. Wide-eyed and wild, with their nostrils flaring, they gallop fast, snorting and kicking up dust.

"Mr. Barley's new steer," Cub says as if I haven't figured this out. "What are they freaked about?"

The answer—a yellow blur—shoots out through the hedge opening faster than a racehorse comes out of a starting gate. My fear at what the blond streak is wrestles with my excitement at seeing him home again. "Dead End!"

G.D. pales.

Cub flushes red and points. "They're headin' for the road!"

CRASH! The steer and dog plow through Mr. Barley's old rail fence as if it were toothpicks held together with dental floss.

"Jeez!" Cub pulls at his hair again. "If that dog is wounded, it sure isn't slowin' him down any!"

At the same time, stocky Mr. Barley, in his dirt-smudged baseball cap, shoots through the opening in the hedge. He stops, staring with his mouth open at the smashed and splintered fence. After a half minute, he turns to G.D., Cub, and me. "I heard yellin'." He looks back at the field. "Did I see a dog chasing my steer?"

My mouth moves, but no words come out. Cub just stares at the shattered fence.

"That's a freezer full of beef goin' down the road," Mr. Barley announces, his voice cracking with his growing panic. "I spent two paychecks on that meat."

"Good-bye hamburger. Good-bye sirloin," Cub mutters for my ears only.

"Did you get a look at that dog?" Mr. Barley comes toward us, breathing hard now, his face rash-red and as strained as a balloon about to pop. "I bet it's one of those pack dogs everyone's been talkin' about." Fred looks right at me, his expression hard. "Where's your dog?"

G.D. blinks as if he isn't sure what he's seen. I hold my breath, hoping with everything I have that he and Cub don't rat out Dead End.

Flustered and frantic, Mr. Barley pulls at the visor of his baseball cap as he turns on his heels, not waiting for anyone to answer his question. "I'm calling Sheriff Hawks. We've got to go after that dog and round up my steer before they're fit for nothing but beef jerky." He jogs back the way he came, a bobbing barrel in overalls, moving faster than I've ever seen him go.

G.D. still gapes at the fence. "Never would have thought Dead End would do anything like that." Shaking his head, slumped and deflated, G.D. works his cane toward the ranch. "Guess you were right, Dill. Bob must not have our dog. Still, we got more than our share of trouble. Lyon won't keep a pooch that chases animals."

"Or kills them," Cub mutters.

I plant my riding boot hard on his foot for that.

"*Oouuff!* Dill!"

G.D. crosses the yard, slower than slow. "I wish I could have taken Dead End to that shelter," he mutters without looking back at us.

When he steps inside, I start for the bikes. "Come on," I call to Cub. "We've got to get to Dead End." But then the telephone rings inside the ranch. Could it be Mr. Kryer again? Or maybe someone else who's seen a yellow dog on the run? I only hesitate a second before I fly into the house. There, I pass G.D. and throw myself at the telephone on the wall at the far end of the kitchen. "Hello?"

"Hey, Dill, it's Tucker Hunter."

"Oh, hi . . ." I suddenly picture Crossfire's bridle on a bale instead of in the tack room. My heart begins thudding.

In the same moment, G.D. makes his way into the kitchen, looking as frail and as delicate as a dried leaf. Cub comes up behind him.

"Remember what I told you about that dog Bob

Kryer trapped in his barn?" Ms. Hunter's voice sounds too serious.

"Yes, ma'am."

G.D. makes his way across the kitchen. Cub pushes up beside me, and mouths *Who is it?*

"Well," Ms. Hunter continues, "Bob just discovered that the dog has escaped. It dug a hole deep enough to squeeze out of and crawled under the stall door."

"Oh?" I picture Dead End's pink-scraped nose. My heart somehow goes to my ears where it thumps a wild rhythm. Even the sweet scent of Mom's blueberry muffins doesn't calm me.

Ms. Hunter sighs. "The sheriff is organizing a huge search for this dog and offering a reward for anyone who brings it in, dead or alive."

My head begins spinning. I nod to show that I've heard her—as if she can see me. The oven timer starts beeping, announcing that the muffins are done.

As Cub pulls them from the oven, G.D. studies me like he knows something isn't good. But instead of hanging around to question me, he works his cane in a bobbing crawl, out of the kitchen. He heads toward his room, and doesn't even seem to care about breakfast.

"Sheriff Hawks wants to talk to your dad about this," Ms. Hunter tells me. "I'm not sure why. Is he there?"

"No," I say, hoping my voice doesn't sound shaky.

"I'll tell him you called. And I got to go," I stammer, watching G.D. move down the hall.

"Oh, okay, Dill."

She barely gets out *good-bye* before I hang up. "Come on, Cub." I head for the back door. "That dog Mr. Kryer caught has escaped."

Cub drops the muffin tin. It hits the stove top with a loud, metallic clank. "Escaped?"

I throw myself back outside instead of answering and grab my bike. Cub follows me. "We got to get Dead End before someone mistakes him for the dog Mr. Kryer captured," I explain.

"Dill, the man had your dog," Cub says in a short and impatient tone, accusing Dead End for at least the third time in two days—three more times than necessary.

Instead of telling him to clap his trap shut, I take off on my bike, tearing down the road with him close behind me. But as we come around the bend near his driveway, he skids to a clanking, rubber-burning stop smack in front of Donny and Danny, his oldest brothers. As much as we need to find Dead End, Cub can't pass his family.

Donny drops his shovel, straightens, and smiles at me. "Hey, Dill. Good to see you."

As worried as I am about the pooch, I thank the heavens that my suddenly weak legs don't give out and leave me face-down on the road. With dirt in my teeth.

Cub's father, who is standing beside the Petersons' idling silver pickup truck, turns and throws me that droopy-eyed pity look that I hate worse than people telling me how I should go to Fairfax. If the minister asks me one more time when I want to talk about Mom, I'll shrug again, and try not to scream *NEVER!*

"Cub, Dill," he says in his creamy-smooth tone. "Did you see a dog chasing steer?"

"Dogs? Steer?" My voice squeaks. Cub's father can probably read my guilt like oversized print.

Mr. Herb Peterson leans out of the pickup. Bald as a boiled egg, his head shines in the sun. "I didn't get a good look, but I think I saw a white or yellow dog."

The minister's forehead crinkles. "Your dog still at your house, Dill?"

Grateful that Cub hasn't told the minister anything about Dead End, I force a grin and nod, hoping that head bobbing doesn't count as a lie. By some miracle, Cub's father accepts this and turns back to Mr. Peterson.

Shaking his head and grumbling his disappointment with me under his breath, Cub climbs off his bike and pushes it over to his brothers (who make a set, each with the Bayer summer buzz cut). I follow, doing my best not to gawk at Donny.

Cub, still ripe-apple red, tries to act calm. "Where'd that dog chasin' the steer go?"

"Mr. Peterson thinks they ran onto our property," Donny tells us in his deep voice.

Danny tips his head at the Emerald Hill Sheep Farm sign on the door of Herb Peterson's truck. "He thinks the dog is one of the mutts that killed his prize sheep."

My throat dries up.

"Let's take a look around your property," Mr. Peterson says to the minister. "Before I call the sheriff."

"Sounds good." The minister moves to the passenger side of the Peterson truck and opens the door. "Boys, finish laying the gravel while I'm gone."

"Yes, Sir," Donny answers.

As the truck peels out, Danny turns on Cub. "You know something about that dog they're looking for." Danny grins, glances at Donny. "Check out the runt's face. He's guilty red and ready to explode."

"We got to go," I croak.

"Don't go getting attached to a dog the way you did to Blackie's pup," Donny warns Cub. Then Donny lifts his shovel. "Now get out of here before I make you shovel stone."

Cub throws himself back onto his bike and spins out.

"And Dill," Donny adds, "let us know if you need anything. Anything at all. Okay?"

Even though just the sniff of sympathy gnaws on my nerves, I force a half-smile and mutter *sure*. For Donny. Then I pedal hard to catch up with Cub.

"They'll tell my dad I'm hiding somethin'," he says when I reach him.

"No, family sticks by you when there's trouble," I point out, handing him Mom's words and hoping with all I have that they're true. "Come on. Let's go to the stable. Maybe Dead End went that way."

• • •

Breathing heavy and running hot, we barely step into the barn when Ms. Hunter comes at us, her long, red braid swinging. "Hey, Dill. Hey, Cub." She smiles easy. "Dill, could you please clean out the horse trailer? Jerry will be taking it to Ohio to pick up show horses I bought last week."

Since I can't say *no* to her, I glance at Cub. His nod says that he'll keep looking for Dead End. "Sure," I answer. "I'll clean out that trailer right away."

161

"I knew I could count on you." She starts to walk away, grinning over her shoulder at me. "How would you like to help me with these new horses? I'd like you to ride them all and see what they can do."

My face explodes into a smile. I sputter because words flat out leave me.

Cub laughs and pushes my arm as Ms. Hunter turns a corner. "Nice."

"Dill riding Ms. Hunter's new horses." Skeeter steps out of the tack room. "Doesn't that figure." He grips his silver-handled crop in a white-knuckled fist as he glares at Cub and then me.

Cub clenches his own fists. "What's it to you, *Skeeter*? Jealous because Ms. Hunter knows Dill is a better rider than you?"

Skeeter glares at Cub with a look that says *eat horse manure and die*. Then he turns to me, his eyes narrowing. "Miss Hunter just feels sorry for you because your . . ."

"Shut your trap," I shout. "I swear, Skeeter, I'll . . ."

Cub grabs my arm, cutting off my threat. "Don't let him know he's getting to you, Dill," he whispers quick into my ear.

Too late. From now until the end of time, Skeeter will be reminding me of why Ms. Hunter feels sorry for me.

"You haven't mucked out my horse's stall yet, Dill,"

the Mosquito adds in a taunting tone. "And Miss Velvet needs her hooves picked, too. Now." His left eye twitches in a kind of warning.

"Why don't you take a hoof pick and . . . ?"

"Dill!" Cub jabs me with his elbow. "Come on. We've got better things than loser insects to worry about."

I scowl at Skeeter, knowing I can't risk him opening his big mouth about Dead End to Ms. Hunter. "I'll take care of Miss Velvet *after* I clean the trailer."

"No. Do it now!" Skeeter jabs the silver handle of his crop at me, barely missing my nose. "I told Ms. Hunter, Jerry Smoothers, and everyone in this stable how we're buddies now." Skeeter's face tips down in what I'd call embarrassment as he says this. For a split second, I get what Mom meant when she said the kid needed to be included. But then he lifts his face again, squinting at me with fresh meanness. "So, don't argue with me, *pal*. Unless you want me to tell Ms. Hunter about the dog I saw you with."

I glare back at him, picturing myself cramming his crop down his throat.

Cub points past Skeeter. "Stubs!"

He wheels around, waving his crop. Cub laughs so hard that he bends over. I grab the chance, turn a corner, and head down the aisle toward Miss Velvet's stall, hoping with all I have that Mr. Smoothers doesn't catch me running. I'm thinking Cub can search for Dead End while I take care of Skeeter's horse, to keep the kid quiet. And then I'll deal with the trailer.

But I barely lead Miss Velvet into the aisle, clip rope lines to either side of her halter, and pull my hoof pick from my back pocket when Ms. Hunter's voice fills the barn. "Cub! Call Dr. Kitt and the sheriff! Tell them to get here fast!" Before he can ask why, Ms. Hunter comes around the corner and right at me.

I freeze, stunned that Ms. Hunter, of all people, is running here. "What's going on?"

She ducks under the rope lines attached to Miss Velvet's halter and continues toward the back entrance. "Dogs just attacked Socrates and Plato!" Her voice quivers.

A sharp *ping* rings out as the hoof pick falls from my hand and hits the floor.

"Dogs." Skeeter slides up behind me. "Friends of yours, I bet, Dill."

"Shut your trap," I warn in my meanest voice before taking off after Ms. Hunter.

• • •

Outside, Jerry Smoothers is kneeling by the riding ring.

"Jerry, what happened?" Ms. Hunter's voice sounds weak and wobbly, as if she's going to cry.

He looks up, breathing hard, his eyes soft for a change, from where he leans over the fallen goat beside the gate. His lips quiver slightly, almost unnoticeably. "Two dogs ran the goats until they were exhausted, then separated them," he says between heaving breaths. He glances down at the goat and strokes the top of his head. Maybe Ms. Hunter is right about him being nicer than he seems. "One of those flea bags attacked Plato."

My hands start shaking. "Are you sure?" I struggle to keep my panic out of this question. "I mean, I didn't hear any barking or . . ."

"I chased them off myself," Jerry snaps, "but not soon enough. And there was more growling and snarling than barking. You wouldn't have heard it from inside the barn."

Ms. Hunter swoops down, and strokes the goat's face. "My poor, poor Plato."

I wince at the ripped, oozing wound on his neck.

A trembling goat bleat echoes out from within the stable.

Ms. Hunter's head lifts. "Socrates got back to their stall. Thank goodness for that."

Socrates cries again. Plato calls back—a weak and

pitiful sound. He tries to stand, but Jerry Smoothers holds him down.

"Let's carry him to his stall, Jerry," Ms. Hunter says. "He'll feel more secure inside, with Socrates."

Together, they lift and slowly carry the wounded goat back to the stable. He fusses only a little, seeming to know these two are trying to help.

Cub meets us in the doorway, clutching Ms. Hunter's cell phone. "Dr. Kitt is on his way and . . . Look at his neck." Cub drops the phone, and then smacks his hands over his nose and mouth. "I might throw up," he mumbles through his fingers.

Ms. Hunter and Jerry disappear into the stable with Plato. When they're out of hearing range, Cub pushes a crumpled page at me. "Skeeter shoved this my way."

The note crinkles in my hands. "After Dill picks Miss Velvet's hooves," I read aloud, "BOTH OF YOU better muck out her stall. Then we're going to see a movie. My mother will drive us."

"What?" I can hardly believe this. "*Movies?* Did he get kicked in the head by his horse?"

Cub clenches his fists. "I'm not sittin' through any movie with that Mosquito."

"Me, neither." Even though I can almost hear Mom reminding me that Skeeter is a lost pup that needs a pack, I can't take even the thought of hanging out with him. Ever.

I keep reading. "And remember, Dill has to back out of the horse show or I'll tell everyone your secret."

"That's it. Manure's gonna be dumped over his head," Cub snarls. "I'm gonna . . ."

A familiar dog yip interrupts. Cub and I look at each other with wide eyes. I grab the sleeve of his T-shirt. "Did that sound like Dead End to you?"

CHAPTER 12

PLENTY OF TROUBLE

"YOU SEE ANYTHING?" AS USUAL, JERRY Smoothers's question comes out as a demand. "I thought I heard a dog." His hand becomes a rigid visor over his eyes. He scowls as he scans the riding ring, the woods, and the path that leads into the trees.

When Cub squints at that trail, he stiffens. His cheeks flush that *we're in trouble* red that I'm getting real tired of seeing.

Trying to stay calm, I glance back at Jerry. "I don't see anything," I tell him, relieved that this isn't a lie.

"Stay here. Keep looking," he snaps. "I'll call the sheriff." Then he limps back to the barn, grumbling something about mangy mutts and how much trouble they cause.

The man barely disappears when Cub grabs my arm, points at some low pine tree branches that are shaking and brushing the edge of the riding path. A black nose scraped pink, attached to a yellow muzzle, pokes out from the tree skirt. Brown eyes that broadcast guilt peer

168

at Cub and me from between green needles. My heart near beats through my chest. "Dead End," I whisper, as I start for the tree.

Cub grabs my arm. "Startle that dog and he'll run from here to China."

So I swallow my urge to sprint and move with Cub, as slow as cold molasses. "He's one sad pooch," I say as we get closer.

"Sad? Dill, Plato just got *attacked*. What does that tell you?"

I don't want to answer, can't bring myself to speak. I glance back at the barn to be sure Jerry hasn't come back out, and then I drop to my knees. I stare into Dead End's eyes and see a familiar sadness called mourning.

"It's okay," I say after a moment. "I know you're sorry for chasing those steer." I swallow hard. "And you didn't go after the goats, did you? You came here to be with people going about their day as if everything is fine. I know."

Dead End whines, inches toward me, keeping his head down and his tail low.

Cub mutters something under his breath, but then bunches up his face as the pooch moves even closer. "His nose—it's covered in blood and dirt!"

"That blood is from a cut." I point. "See. On his muzzle."

"That blood isn't from any cut, Dill." Cub shakes his head as if he's been given the worst news ever. "His paws are all filthy, too. Like he's dug out of some place." Cub pulls the collar of his T-shirt up and over his mouth and nose. "And he stinks again."

Cub barely spits this out when the raw stench hits my nose like a freight train. As if this isn't bad enough, he points at more dried blood crusted around a wide, wet gash across Dead End's shoulder. The wound glistens red and meaty under a dirty crust.

Cub pulls back, and makes a strangled sound through the T-shirt. "Dead End is the dog that Mr. Jonas clipped when he took aim at the pack going after his sheep."

Before I can argue, Dead End slides on his belly, farther out from under the tree. I inch closer to him, lean forward, offer him my hand. He licks my palm and gives happy dog grunts, his tail thumping. Blood or no blood, I want to hug and kiss this crazy pooch, smother him in pets and tell him that I understand his need to run from what has happened. "You're a good dog trying to deal with a whole lot of hurt," I tell him, looking into his face, understanding.

Cub snorts. "Good dogs don't chase steer, kill groundhogs, and . . ." He stops when I shoot him my coldest glare.

"Never mind," I growl. "Let's get him home."

Cub kicks at the ground. "How? We can't go past the stable with him."

"We'll go through the woods, follow the old, abandoned train tracks. It'll take forever, but at least no one will see us."

"We need a collar and a leash." Cub whips off his old belt with the extra holes punched in it. By some miracle, his baggy, handed-down shorts don't drop to his ankles as he fastens the belt about Dead End's neck in a makeshift collar. The spare length becomes a short leash.

Dead End's tail stops wagging. He sneezes.

• • •

The next morning, early, the hinges of the barn door creak when Cub pulls the thing closed behind him, leaving Dead End inside. Cleaned up and curled into a doughnut on his blanket, with the new bone beside him, the pooch has just finished licking his wounds and is digesting his breakfast along with his favorite cookies—cranberry-raisin—which I'd baked for him, using Mom's recipe. "We've got to keep him out here until I can figure out how to explain his wounds." My voice shakes as I picture Mom petting Socrates and Plato. She always went out of her way to find them when she came to the stable to watch my riding lessons. She'd bring those goats hand-fuls of grain or garden vegetables donated by Cub.

Cub fusses with twine and wire, twisting and knot-ting it over the handle as if the door needs to hold closed against a herd of stampeding elephants. "Dill, yesterday Plato was attacked by a dog at the same time that Dead End was at the stable. Think about that."

In no mood to consider this for even half a minute, I head for the ranch.

Once he's secured the door closed, Cub scuffs up behind me. "Even if he didn't attack Plato, your dog's in plenty of trouble."

We pass Mom's garden, the weeds growing tall and strong without G.D.'s daily maintenance. "I've got to tell G.D. that Dead End's back and . . ." The ring of the kitchen telephone, as startling as a fire alarm, keeps me from saying anymore. I bolt. Cub follows, closer than my shadow.

"Hello," I say, breathless from lunging across the kitchen to snatch the telephone receiver from the wall. At the same time, my gaze finds G.D.'s bedroom door at the end of the hall, sealed closed because he is sleeping late again, which makes my chest heavy.

Cub watches me without blinking.

"Dill, I'm glad you're there," the voice on the phone says.

172

Cub pushes my shoulder. "Who is it?"

I cover the receiver with my palm. "Ms. Hunter." Cub's eyes go wide. I slide my hand off the telephone. "How's Plato?"

Ms. Hunter lets out a deep breath. "Stitched up. Dr. Kitt thinks he'll be fine." She sounds relieved. "Listen, Dill, are you okay? Jerry said that you and Cub left yesterday afternoon even though he'd told you to watch for the dogs that attacked Plato. That's not like you. I know we have a riding lesson later, but I wanted to talk to you before you got busy with Crossfire and your stable duties."

Cub pushes me again. "What's she sayin'?"

I wave at him to hush.

"And you left Crossfire's bridle out after your riding lesson. You didn't clean the trailer, either. You've never turned your back on stable rules and instructions before." She sighs again. "You're not yourself, Dill. I'm worried about you. I know you're going through a very tough time, but . . ."

"I'm fine," I spit out to stop her from going on. But I feel bad right off. How can I lie to Ms. Hunter?

After a minute of silence that feels more like a year, she sighs. "If there is anything that I can do, Dill," she says in a softer tone, "I hope that you'll come to me."

"Thanks. I'll be better about instructions and . . ." All

at once, the image of Miss Velvet tied to the rope lines in the middle of an aisle where I'd left her yesterday pops into my head, and makes me choke on the rest of my sentence. Ms. Hunter must know that someone broke one of her most important stable rules, and left a horse out of its stall and unattended. "That mess with Plato shook me up," I throw out.

"I understand. Don't worry. Sheriff Hawks will catch the dogs in that pack."

This almost makes me gag, but I manage to get out a last apology before I hang up. And as I do, my hand hits a note taped to the body of the telephone where Lyon, Mom, and I have always left notes for each other. Lyon even bought special self-sticking note squares to save Mom and me the trouble of dealing with tape.

Lyon, G.D.'s wobbly handwriting reads. *We got to talk about Dead End. Wake me when you get in. Pop*

Cub steps closer, reads the note. "That's it. We're dead."

I rip the note from the telephone, stuff it into my pocket, then pull a pencil and paper from a drawer. *G.D.,* I write. *Dead End is back. Everything will be great. I have to go to the stable, but I'll be back soon. PLEASE don't tell Lyon about Dead End before we talk! Love, Dill*

Cub eyes the note. "Have to go to the stable?"

"Yeah . . . uh . . ." I clear my throat. "I kind of left Miss Velvet tied up in the aisle in front of her stall yesterday."

"Dill!" Cub grabs his hair, yanks. "That goes against the biggest stable rule ever!"

"No kidding." I hurry to G.D.'s bedroom and slide my note under the door. "I've got to check on Dead End quick, then get back to the stable to figure out what happened—who found that horse and put her away, and who knows about this."

"If Jerry Smoothers saw that horse tied up with no one around, we'll be in two tons of trouble," Cub groans. "Aw, Dill, I don't want to lose my stable job. I love bein' around those animals and . . ." He hesitates. "Wait a second." A grin spreads across his face. "It's Skeeter's horse. *He's* the one who'll get his butt kicked. His mother will blow a vocal cord yellin' at him!"

"Yeah, and that'll make him spitting mad. He'll get back at us by ratting on us about Dead End." I throw myself out the back door and head for the barn. "We'd better hope with everything we've got that someone other than Skeeter or Jerry Smoothers put that horse away."

• • •

The midafternoon Virginia summer heat sends sweat skidding down the back of my neck as Cub and I jog up the stable driveway. "Remind me never to leave my bike here again or . . ." My skin begins prickling—and not from the heat—when I see Mr. Fred Barley's dented and muddy pickup truck parked smack next to Sheriff Hawk's patrol car.

Cub turns to me, wide-eyed. Wiping at his sweaty forehead, he streaks road dust across his skin. "What'll we do now?"

Cub barely gets this out when Skeeter comes busting out of the back of the stable, barreling toward us like a locomotive. The veins in his neck are bulging, his eyes are popping-out angry.

"Someone's got his underwear in a wad," Cub mutters.

"All you want to do is make me look bad!" Skeeter waves his silver-handled crop like he's going to beat us with it. "I just got in trouble because *someone* left my horse tied up in the aisle yesterday." The Mosquito jabs the crop tip into my shoulder. "You left her out on purpose!"

"Don't be an idiot. I did not." I sigh. "Listen, I'm sorry. I'll tell Ms. Hunter that I . . ."

"Too late." Skeeter's knuckles turn white on the crop. "I just did. Two minutes ago. I told her that *you* left Miss Velvet out because *you* were working for me to keep me from telling everyone about your sheep-killing dog."

My hands go for his throat. Skeeter jumps back, waving his stupid crop, begging for me to take it from him and bash it over his fat head. "You can forget about your riding lesson today, Dill. You'll never ride Ms. Hunter's horses again!" He scrambles backwards. "No more horse shows, nothing for you. Serves you right!" He laughs as he runs back into the barn.

"You'd better run!" Cub yells after him.

"Ms. Hunter!" Skeeter's shriek echoes through the barn.

"And he wonders why he has no friends." Cub scowls. "I hope Stubs finds him."

And I wonder how everything could have gone so wrong so fast. If I'd told Lyon the truth about Dead End, would Cub and I be in this mess right now?

"What now?" Cub blinks at me, his eyes giving away his fear.

"I've got to get Dead End out of town quick. I've got to get him to that shelter G.D. talked about." I grab Cub's arm, and pull him back toward our bikes.

• • •

Back at home, my heart is still hammering at about ninety miles an hour as I drop a can of cold soda onto the kitchen table, in front of Cub. Then I go to Dead End, and slide off the twine collar and leash that Cub put on him to bring him inside from the barn. The minute he's free, the silly pooch shakes from nose to tail.

I go down to my knees and wrap my arms around him until I can feel his heart beating. I lay my cheek against the fur of his, not caring what he's been into or how bad he has smelled, but instead, wondering how I'll ever face things head-on.

That's when the door to the garage whips open. "Dill?" Lyon's voice booms, screaming trouble. The door slams behind him.

Cub chokes on his next soda sip. I hold my breath. Dead End turns, his tail making huge circles as he trots across the kitchen to greet Lyon, who stomps toward us with his hands clenched into big fists. Something about the way his dark eyebrows crinkle together gives his anger a frightening sharpness that I've only seen a couple times. The toothpick in his mouth should be in splinters. He pats our dog's head once, quickly, then brushes past him, coming at us.

"You're home real early," I say, cautious. "I haven't even started dinner yet. And G.D. is napping."

Lyon's eyes narrow on me. "Ms. Hunter called me about something she heard."

Cub drops his head into his hands.

"Tell me you haven't been keeping one of those sheep-killing dogs."

"He's not a . . ."

"DYLAN MACGREGOR!" Lyon takes in a deep breath, drags a flattened hand over his face, from his forehead south, to his chin. "Answer the question: Have you been keeping a dog?"

My mouth dries up.

Cub lifts his face, sits up straight. "It's Dead End, Sir."

Lyon jerks as if Cub has slapped him. "What? *Dead End?*"

"He's a good dog," I whine, my voice trickling out thin and desperate. On cue, the pooch comes to my side and nuzzles his scraped nose into my palm.

Lyon turns away from me, and then rakes a hand through his hair. "Good dog? People have lost valuable animals. Neighbors are fighting and demanding that each other's dogs be put to sleep. Farmers are buying guns, traps, and poison!"

"There's no proof that Dead End went after any farm animals. He's never even looked sidelong at a sheep," I blurt out. "You know that. G.D. knows it, too."

Lyon's anger deflates like a popped balloon. "G.D." Staring at his feet, Lyon sighs. "Dill, I can't deal with Dead End right now. We need to talk about G.D. I was getting ready to come home when Ms. Hunter called me."

Why does his tone drop? Suddenly, I want his anger back—anything but his terrible sadness.

He turns back to me. Sucking in a long breath, he lifts his face. He's only looked this worn out, beaten down, once before—when he told me of how he'd taken Mom to the hospital in the middle of the night. "Doc Kerring thinks the hospital is the best place for G.D." Lyon sighs, his toothpick drooping. "I've come home to take him there."

"NO!" My tone flares up like a freshly lit match, but inside I'm shaking. The tears are coming.

"I'm sorry, Dill, but G.D. agreed to go this time." Lyon's voice is cold and flat. Mom once told me not to ever let this chilly distance fool me. She said Lyon gets closed off and winter-like when he's trying hard not to feel.

He turns away from me, and moves down the short hall, toward G.D.'s room. "Lyon! Don't!"

Cub's mouth drops open. He starts pacing, pulling at his hair. And I'm suddenly hating that he has to see all this.

Lyon pushes G.D.'s bedroom door open. The hinges creak. "Pop?" Lyon's voice gets gentle, the way I know it best. "You ready?"

G.D.'s thin mumble drifts into the kitchen, but I can't make out his words. Feet shuffle, slow. G.D.'s rings jingle as he hobbles into the kitchen, leaning on Lyon as well as that Civil War cane.

"G.D.?" My lips tremble. My eyes begin to burn. But I don't want to cry, not in front of Cub. Not in front of anybody.

G.D. holds up a bony hand in a stop signal. "Got to go this time, girl."

"But Dead End's back," I mutter as I stroke the dog's head. I blink quickly, using every bit of strength I have to keep from exploding into tears that might never stop.

Smiling large, his tail wagging, the pooch trots over to G.D., who drops one fragile hand to the yellow head. "Take care of him for me," G.D. says, his voice unsteady, a trickle. "Got to face this head-on."

"Come on, Pop." Lyon tugs at G.D.

His hand moves in slow motion from Dead End to the faded baseball cap that I've seen a million times during all his visits over the years. A hat that he'd picked up at some championship game in Chicago. He pulls at its visor, as if this can hide his moist and red-rimmed eyes.

Then Lyon guides G.D. across the rest of the kitchen and the family room. Dead End returns to me, stays close. At the garage door, Lyon hesitates and looks back before leaving, his eyes full of a pain I've seen only once before. "I'm sorry, Dill. We'll talk about Dead End when I get home."

After Lyon turns away from me, I go to the doorway. Slow as tar, Lyon and G.D. move to Lyon's pickup truck. There, Lyon lifts G.D. into the passenger side as if he is nothing more than a bundle of sticks. In a blink, he's Mom sitting there, frail as a sparrow. Like G.D., she'd been unable to fight against being carted off to the cold, metallic county hospital with all its needles and poisonous drugs.

My last chance to run at the truck and scream at Lyon to stop sits right in front of me, but I can't move. Unlike Mom, G.D. looks peaceful with his back against the seat, his face to the sun, his eyes closed.

CHAPTER 13

ROOM 524

Cub kicks at my bedroom doorway, but doesn't move one toe past it into my room. He never does. "I told my mom about your granddad goin' to the hospital. She sent over a casserole for your dinner. Chicken and green beans, I think. It's on the counter. I told her you still hadn't touched the lasagna she sent over after your mom . . ." He catches himself, and rams his toe into the doorjamb. "Anyway, I told her you already had plenty of food in your freezer, but she still wanted me to bring over that dish."

"Tell her *thanks,* again."

Cub hesitates, and sucks in a big breath. "My dad says you should come talk to him. I think he's right, Dill."

"Tell the minister *thanks anyway.*"

Cub kicks harder at the doorway. "I, uh, didn't see Lyon's truck in the driveway."

"He hasn't come home from the hospital." My insides go quivery. I turn away from Cub, and glide Mom's

183

opened bottle of gardenia perfume under my nose to bring her back for a moment.

"Dill, you got to admit that G.D. hasn't been looking good. Maybe the doctors will help this time."

I glance at the more than twenty postcards I've spread over my bedroom floor, notes sent by G.D. from all the different places he'd visited during his years of zigzagging over the country.

Cub clears his throat. "Not everyone dies when they go to the hospital. My mom has been there lots."

"Pushing out babies is different." I inhale gardenia again, almost dumping what remains of the perfume when the telephone rings suddenly.

Cub hops back, out of my way, as I jump up from the floor (after securing the top on the perfume bottle) and bolt through the doorway, heading for the kitchen. "Hello?"

"Dill, it's your dad."

Lyon hasn't called himself *dad* since the morning he told me that Mom was gone.

"I'm still at the hospital." His voice is steady, unreadable.

No matter how hard I imagine stuffing the anger with Lyon's name on it inside the jar deep inside me and sealing the lid tight, the fury still seeps out and foams up.

"I'm coming to get you." He doesn't leave an inch for argument. "You need to be here."

The receiver clatters onto the kitchen floor. I grab the twine leash and collar from the counter, and slip it over Dead End's head. He jumps up from his bed, sensing my urgency. He doesn't even have time to sneeze as I run for the back door, abandoning Cub and his mother's casserole.

A second before I launch myself and the dog out of the house, I hear Cub scramble for the phone. "Hello? Mr. MacGregor? It's me, Sir. Cub."

• • •

Twenty minutes might have passed before the barn door creaks open and late afternoon sunlight fills the place. Blinking, I pause from trying to knot and tie fresh bailing twine into a makeshift collar and leash. I squint at Cub's dark, scrawny form. Beside me, Dead End pants and smiles, thumping his tail.

"Knew you'd be out here with him." Cub pulls the barn door closed. And then he crinkles his forehead at the mess in my hands. "What are you trying to do there?"

"Make a stronger collar and leash for this dog."

When Cub takes the twine from me, I return to stroking Dead End's head. "He knows something's wrong," I say. "He hasn't been sniffing for food, hasn't even checked my pockets for cookies." My voice wavers. Another fat tear plops onto the yellow fur.

Cub shifts from foot to foot, working his magic on the string. "That dog sure has turned everything upside down around here."

"Lyon turned everything upside down." *By taking Mom to the hospital,* I don't add.

"You got to stop blaming him," Cub tells me. "It's not his fault your mom got sick. It's not his fault she . . ."

"I told him not to take her to the hospital," I spit, cutting Cub off.

"The hospital isn't what happened to her, Dill." Cub sighs, smart enough to let the subject drop. "Dill, Lyon wants you to . . ."

"I know what he wants," I snap, interrupting Cub again. Dead End stops panting, and looks up at me with his head tipped to one side. "I'm not going to that stupid hospital." I sniff, and wipe at my eyes.

Cub's hands pause from looping and knotting as he squints at me. "Dill, you should be with Lyon and your granddad. That's what your mom would want."

I stiffen.

"G.D. would tell you to *face this head-on.*" Cub stares at me without blinking. "It's time you did that." He hands me the new bailing twine collar and leash, double knotted in places. Dead End stops panting. His tail drops, goes limp.

Cub stops kicking at the floor. "You can't bring a dog to the hospital, Dill."

I drag the back of my hand under my nose. "I'm not. I'm taking care of him the way G.D asked me to. I've got a plan."

Cub looks confused, like he can't decide between being excited or scared about this.

"I'm going to bring this dog to my room for the night and then sneak him off to the stable early tomorrow morning, before dawn. If we hide in the back of the horse trailer, we can catch a ride with Jerry Smoothers when he goes to Ohio." I slip the twine collar over Dead End's head. "I'm sorry," I whisper to him. "It's only for a while." The pooch sneezes, of course, and then he shakes with everything he has.

I stroke his face, looking into his chocolate eyes. "It isn't safe for you here anymore with everyone thinking that you're a sheep killer." I start toward the door, the twine leash wrapped around my wrist.

"After you get Dead End inside," Cub says, "we'll go to the hospital together."

• • •

An hour later, Donny pulls his rattling hunk of a pickup truck up to the front of the big county hospital. "I'll meet you two in the parking lot," he says, giving me a droopy, sympathetic look.

"Thanks for the ride," Cub says. Then his hand tugs on my wrist. "Come on, Dill. Room five hundred and twenty-four."

He pulls me up the sidewalk and through the front doors, apparently clueless that my feet feel as heavy as cinder blocks. All tucked in and brushed off (and as stubborn as ever), he drags me through the carpeted reception area, into wide, bleach-clean hallways soaked in white light. My hands shake and my insides quiver as images of Mom, lying in a bed, force themselves into my head. To fight these off, I try to picture her humming and digging in her garden with Dead End smiling and panting beside her.

Cub herds me into an elevator. My knees go weak when he hits a button and the machinery hums. One by one, numbers light over the door at each floor as a bell chime spells out *NO . . . TURNING . . . BACK . . . NOW,* a word at a clang.

When the number five lights, the elevator stops and the doors slide open, letting in the smells of rubbing alcohol and antiseptic. I push my wrist to my face, but the hospital smells overpower Mom's gardenia scent. In the hallways and rooms that I can see, fragile patients in hospital-gown uniforms look tired of facing life head-on.

Cub gives me a gentle push, then a harder one, guiding me, making me step into another white-lighted hall. "Room five hundred and twenty-four."

"I, I can't," I squeak.

Nurses move like robots, crisscrossing the corridors between the rooms and a station in the center of the floor. One nurse steers a woman in a wheelchair past us. This patient has Mom's pale, drawn face. The hopelessness that comes at the end shows in her dull eyes and quiet lips.

To ease a rising panic, I picture Mom brushing Dead End from nose to tail while whispering sweet words into his ears. I see her taking him with her to do the grocery shopping and banking. He would go almost everywhere that she went, sitting shotgun in her old Jeep. But these cheerful images don't last. The sterile hospital air smothers them in the same way that it snuffs out her gardenia perfume.

Cub nudges me. Too worn out to fight him off, I keep moving, and focus on the shiny floor and the light glistening on chrome wheelchairs parked along the wall. I'd have concentrated on bedpans to keep from seeing any more patients looking the way Mom had looked in this place.

As Cub slows, a nurse steps out from a room in front of us. She looks at someone behind Cub and me. "No more visitors for him," she says in a soft voice, shaking her head in a way that seems too final.

My heart stops.

"Okay," a female from behind us answers. "Is his son still with him?"

I look up at the numbers over the door. *524.*

"Miss, that's a private room. . . ."

Lyon sits beside the hospital bed, his elbows on the edge of the mattress, his hands folded and his head down. G.D. lies as still as a statue. His frail body, almost lost beneath the blankets, looks like a shell without its snail. He doesn't smile, doesn't frown. His face has lost the pain-pinched expression.

"Mom." The word, no more than a whimper, squeezes itself from my strangled throat without my permission.

Lyon whips around. He blinks his red, wet eyes, and then drags his big mitt of a hand over his drawn face. "Dill." His voice shakes and his lips tremble. "The doctors and nurses made him comfortable. He's been suffering at home. He . . ."

I back off from his words until my shoulders slam into the wall beside the door. Then, turning, I throw myself out of the room and run down the hall, back the way Cub and I had come.

Cub and the nurses become brief blurs in the white-lighted tunnel of this corridor.

"Dill, wait!"

Lyon's voice makes me run harder. I throw myself into a stairwell and then fly over the steps. When I get to the main floor, I sprint across the lobby and out of the hospital.

CHAPTER 14

OVER

"DILL, IT'S CRAZY TO TAKE DEAD END ALL THE WAY out to that shelter G.D. talked about." Cub grinds the toe of his unlaced work boot into the floor outside my bedroom. "What're you gonna do when, or if, you get there?"

While trying to ignore the headache that is hammering my skull, I finger the photo of Mom and Lyon in my pocket, checking to be sure it's still there. My swollen eyes have gone blurry from too many tears. "The last thing G.D. asked . . ." Dead End snuffles and then licks my cheek. I wrap my arms around him and bury my face in his thick neck fur as a fresh sob, heavy and hot, pushes up my throat, sucking up the little bit of energy I have left. "He asked me to take care of Dead End," I say when I get a grip on myself and lift my face. "He knows this is what Mom would have wanted, too." I stuff a tube of antibiotic ointment and a box of bandages for Dead End's wounds into G.D.'s leather knapsack. Weathered as an old boot, the thing holds his smell. A scent something like the inside of a cedar chest full of saddle leather. Whenever he paused from wandering to visit with us, he always had this knapsack. It's hard to picture him traveling without it.

Sniffing, I wipe at my nose, and then drop and reach under my bed for the coffee can that I've been using as a bank, stuffing my stable pay away, saving for a horse or even a stable of my own someday. "I'm going to hide Dead End at that shelter until all the dog pack trouble blows over."

Cub plants his hands on his hips. "How are you gonna get across the country?"

I pull out the coffee can and sit up. "I told you: Tomorrow morning, when Jerry Smoothers heads to Ohio to pick up those horses for Ms. Hunter, Dead End and I will be hiding in the trailer." My fingers pluck at the two hundred and sixty-two dollars in the can. Fifty-two cents roll on the bottom as Dead End pokes at the can with his nose.

"What about getting from Ohio to that shelter? G.D. said it's in Utah. That's clear across the country."

"We'll walk and catch rides the way G.D. used to do when he stopped driving, before he came to live with us." The brochure and map crinkle as I pull them from the back pocket of my jeans. "I found these in G.D.'s trunk." Cub leans into my room, squinting as I point at the brochure. "The address is right here."

"Dill, that shelter is too far away. It's not safe to *catch rides*."

"If I don't go, Dead End could be . . ." Unable to say *shot* or *put to sleep,* I return the map and brochure to my back pocket and then stuff my savings into my front pockets.

"What about Lyon?"

I grab my jean jacket and put it beside G.D.'s knapsack. "He'll probably be relieved to be rid of me. You know, like he's relieved to be rid of Seymour the goat, the rabbits, and Double and Trouble, the cats."

"You're wrong, Dill."

"Whatever," I choke out, my head spinning, my chest tight. "I'll call Lyon when Dead End and I get to Ohio."

Cub shakes his head, looking disappointed.

"Come with me." I stare smack into his eyes. "Why not? You'll get away from all your chores, your brothers, and your responsibilities—you know, the garden and all the church functions."

Cub squirms, not looking at me straight on. "Donny and Danny never told my dad or Mr. Peterson about Dead End." And then he shrugs. "That garden and all those church functions aren't all that bad." Cub stays focused on his unlaced boots. "Truth is, watchin' you these last few months, seein' how bad it is to be without a whole family . . ." He hesitates, jabs his toe at the molding again. "Guess you've shown me a thing or two about appreciation, Dill."

"Good." My voice has an edge of resentment. "It's about time you realize what you have." My envy is raw and obvious now because I'm too worn out to tamp it down any longer.

Neither of us says another word for a long moment. Cub shifts from foot to foot. When Dead End goes to him and pushes at his hand, asking for pets, Cub ruffles the dog's ears and takes in a big breath. "I don't think you should leave, Dill. Runnin' off isn't going to make this mess go away."

I look away from him because something tells me he's right. Still, I stuff another bottle of water, a paper plate, and a small plastic container (for Dead End's food and drink) into the knapsack and yank the zipper closed. "I got to go" is all I can get out.

• • •

I close Dead End and myself into my room early, and crawl into bed before Lyon gets home so we don't have to see him. And by some miracle, he leaves me be, doesn't even knock on the door after returning from the hospital.

I don't set my alarm because I don't need to. There's no way sleep will be coming my way tonight. The minutes crawl because I won't breathe easy until Dead End and I are in the trailer, rolling toward Ohio. But eventually, hours later, the pooch and I sneak out of the ranch without getting caught. We make it to the stable by four A.M.

All around the spare stall where we sit hidden behind bales of hay, waiting for the first sign of sunrise, horses snort and stamp. I consider going to Crossfire, but I'm not sure I can take saying good-bye to him. Besides, the stable darkness feels mud-thick. Bats squeak in the rafters. Rats and mice skitter behind the walls.

"Eat up," I tell the dog as I dump kibbles from a plastic bag onto the paper plate. And then I pour water into the plastic container. "Once it's light, we'll go find the trailer."

I barely finish the sentence when Dead End's head pops up from his food. He stops chewing and his ears lift. His body goes rigid.

The door at the front of the barn rolls, sliding open. Slow, booted steps, heavy and too familiar, echo on cement. *Thud . . . thud . . . thud . . .*

Click. Yellow light, more startling than an explosion, fills the stable. "Dill, it's me. Where are you?"

Lyon. Every inch of me goes as stiff as a plank. "Be quiet," I whisper low, stroking Dead End's back. "Be a good dog."

"Dill. I know you're in here. Cub couldn't stand the thought of you running off. He called the house, told me what you're about to do."

My fingers curl as if around that kid's scrawny neck.

"Come on out, talk to me." A long pause. "I know you're upset about G.D., but he'll be okay. Weak from a few health problems that we'll have to cope with, but he'll be home today."

I gasp, leap up, and almost run to Lyon—until Dead End tips his head, questioning me with his big eyes.

Lyon sighs. "Dill . . ." His voice shakes. It never does this. "Come out. Talk to me the way you used to do. Please."

He might as well have stomped on my heart with his huge work boots. Since I can't sit still a second longer, I wipe at my eyes and under my dripping nose. I tie Dead End's leash to the twine of a hay bale because I don't need the dog getting all worked up and excited over seeing Lyon right before we leave. Then I kiss the pink-scraped snout. "Be good. Stay," I whisper in a quivering voice.

He sneezes, thumps his tail.

Hay rustles as I push past bales, wiping leftover tears off my face. I can hear the echo of Lyon's steps, can picture him moving back and forth and side to side in that awkward shuffle that shows he doesn't know what to do with himself.

He turns around when I clear the corner, his dark hair still sleep-messed, his eyes wide and full of fear. He chews hard on the end of a toothpick. Then he shoots at me—a two-hundred-pound bullet in a denim shirt.

"Dill . . ." His voice evaporates as his big arms wrap around me in a bear hug. The old Lyon. He still smells of the hospital, but I don't care. "You're too young to take off, go wandering the way G.D. did," he says into my hair. "And I'm nowhere near ready to let you go."

This sounds like the Lyon from a year ago, before he'd built the wall around himself. "I've got to get Dead End to a safe place," I mumble into his shirt.

Lyon squeezes me tighter. "Running off won't change anything. Haven't you learned that from G.D.?"

"I've got money," I tell him, my voice small.

He releases me, steps back. A dense sigh leaves him. And he wilts some. "Dill, you and I got to start understanding that we have to face some things in order to get them resolved. If our dog has been killing sheep, we've got to deal with that. Folks shouldn't have to worry about protecting their animals from pack dogs. And what about my store? Keeping a dog that kills isn't exactly good for business."

I push away from him. "But Dead End . . ."

Lyon holds up a hand before I can even try to say *is Mom's dog*. The toothpick slides to one side of his mouth. "I don't want to argue." He pushes his fingers back through his hair and sighs again. "Let's make a deal. You and Dead End come home. We'll keep him inside and on a leash until this whole dog pack mess gets resolved. *If* he is *not* a sheep killer, *then* we'll take him back to Sarah Doyle for some retraining, to get him to stop running off. Okay?"

A grin splashes over my whole face and I dance inside. "Deal," I say.

"Okay." Lyon plants a warm kiss on my forehead for the first time in months. His big hand squeezes my shoulder. "Go get our dog."

• • •

"From now on, you'll sleep beside my bed," I tell Dead End as Lyon's truck tires crunch our driveway gravel. "After Lyon fixes your shoulder. He's real good at patching wounds." He should be. He's cleaned and doctored enough of my cuts, scrapes, and banged-up bones. Because Mom had a habit of panicking when I got hurt. She could never stay calm enough to be my nurse.

The dog licks my face. He'd have swung his tail in O's if we'd had the room in the cab. This makes me feel a warmth that has been missing—at least until Cub shoots out of the garage, coming right at the front of Lyon's truck.

Lyon throws the truck into park and leans out of the window. "What're you doing here, son? You should be home, sleeping. The sun is barely up."

"People have been callin'," Cub gasps between panting breaths. "My house. Your house. Skeeter told anyone who'd listen that we've been keeping a sheep killer." Cub turns to me, his face as red as I've ever seen it, his eyes as wide as bottle caps.

I leap out of the truck, slamming the door closed behind me to keep Dead End inside. "Skeeter's lying again! That insect's a blood-sucking liar!"

"There's more." Cub swallows hard, shifting from foot to foot. He glances at Lyon, and then looks back at me. "Sheriff Hawks came by my house last night when no one answered the door here. He's got photographs. One of the farmers took pictures of the dogs goin' after his sheep. You know, for proof." Cub looks at his feet. "One shows a blond husky." He hesitates. "It's Dead End."

My knees turn weak. My hands begin sweating and shaking.

"Now, Ms. Hunter believes Dead End attacked Plato." Cub swallows hard, focusing on Lyon again. "Sheriff Hawks is lookin' for you and Dead End, Sir."

The world begins spinning faster.

"That's it." Lyon's no-nonsense tone echoes in the dark. He throws the truck into reverse, and whips it onto the lawn in a backwards U-turn until the head-lights are pointing at the road.

His words explode in my head: *Dogs that go after livestock should be destroyed.* "Lyon! No! Don't!" I run at his truck, throwing myself in front of it. "You can't take Mom's dog! You can't!"

Lyon leans out the window. His face is rock-hard. "I'm sorry, Dill, but this dog is a threat." His voice booms.

"But he's Mom's dog," I blurt out. Tears leak from my eyes despite my fight to hold them back. "We had a deal! Mrs. Doyle can make him a good dog again!"

"Get out of the way, Dill. Please." When I don't, won't, Lyon throws the truck into reverse again, backs up some, then shifts back into drive and steers wide around me.

I chase that truck with everything I've got. The tears come strong now. "Don't take her! You can't!" My soaked, wet cries get lost in the spitting gravel of our driveway. When I finally stop, breathing hard enough to pop a lung, sobbing to the point of shaking, I watch through blurry eyes as the truck tears down the road. Then I drop to my knees, grab handfuls of gravel and throw them as hard as I can at Lyon and his truck. "I HATE YOU!" I scream as loud as I'm able, my vocal cords close to snapping. "You took Mom away. I didn't even say good-bye. I HATE YOU! I HATE YOU! I HATE YOU!" And I crumple into a limp heap.

Slow, hesitant steps crunch the gravel behind me.

"She's gone," I gasp at Cub in a trembling, snuffling voice. "I mean . . . they're gone."

"I know, Dill." He kicks at the ground, harder than usual. "I'm sorry."

CHAPTER 15 | GOOD DOG

I STARE AT THE PHONE ON THE KITCHEN WALL UNTIL IT stops ringing. In the master bedroom, the answering machine finishes recording a fourth message. With a sigh, I start back to my bedroom.

When I get to the hallway, Cub turns away from the closed door of Lyon's bedroom and comes to meet me, stomping on the ends of his untied laces. "Dill, I think that last call might have been your dad again. His message sounded like it said something about Dr. Kitt and St. Bernard's Animal Shelter."

I shrug, acting like I don't care, and step back into my bedroom. I return to G.D.'s knapsack, in the middle of the floor, and stuff Mom's bottle of gardenia perfume into the side pocket of it. Then I rub at the puffy, raw skin around my eyes. Less than a blink of sleep all night from grieving for G.D. and waiting for the time when Dead End and I could leave the ranch, combined with the drain from this latest drama, has left me feeling as if I've been dragged behind a train from Virginia to

California. But the jar inside me sits empty, the lid blown off from my outburst at Lyon. After all that letting go, the emptiness (despite my tiredness) is clean and fresh—and tastes like relief.

"Lyon has been leaving messages all morning," Cub reminds me, like I don't know this, don't recognize my father's deep voice on the machine in the other room, even if I can't make out his words.

I'd closed the door of the master bedroom when the phone first rang. I don't want to know what Lyon is doing.

"Lyon's either dumping our dog at a shelter or having Dr. Kitt . . ." *put Dead End to sleep* lumps in my throat. My head still aches. Another tidal wave of tears rises behind my eyelids, which feel as thick and as swollen as overcooked pasta.

Cub turns away, sniffing and wiping at his face in quick swipes.

"Why couldn't I convince Dead End to stay here with us?" My voice cracks.

"Maybe G.D. was right, Dill." Cub's voice comes out shaky. "Maybe that dog has been on a mission to find your mom."

I drop my head, push my knuckles against my eyes as if I can plug up the tears. How will I ever tell G.D. what has happened to his four-legged buddy? "I've got to get out of here." I sniff.

"You can't run from a busted heart," Cub says low. "That's not facin' life head-on."

Before I can scream that I don't give a rat's rear end about facing anything head-on, a familiar rumble crawls up the driveway.

Cub turns his head to the sound.

The truck goes quiet. The door to the garage opens, stays that way for a long few minutes, then shuts again, slow. Lyon's boots thump. They're followed by a shuffling of feet. "Dill," Lyon calls. "Where are you?"

Cub heads for the kitchen.

"Hey, Cub." Lyon's voice comes out slow and heavy, tired.

"Hey, Mr. MacGregor, Sir. And . . ." Cub sounds as if the air's being sucked out of him the way his voice trails off.

"Where's Dill?"

I stand and hike the knapsack onto my shoulder. Fighting back more tears, I force myself into the kitchen.

Lyon and his toothpick come at me. "Dill, I'm sorry I had to leave you upset. And I'm sorry I didn't get home sooner. Did you get my messages? I had to drive . . ."

"I don't want to hear it. You took him away. You take everyone I love away—to die."

Everyone freezes, including me. Because *die* isn't a word I've been using. And because at that moment, I see

G.D. at the kitchen table, settling his bone-thin self into his usual chair. "G.D.," I whisper with a smile in my voice. "You're home." I go to him, wrap one gentle arm around his shoulders, and kiss his papery cheek.

He nods, pats my hand with his, gives me back a smile. "Can't keep this old hound down. No ma'am."

When I straighten, Lyon reaches for my shoulders, but I turn away from his hands, still too mad to do business with him. "Dill, you said *die*. You finally said *die*," he breathes, sounding relieved, even pleased.

The word brings on another gush of tears like water from a faucet. Lyon reaches for me again. I turn away, knowing how long he's been waiting to see me cry. His hands hit the knapsack.

G.D. arches his bushy eyebrows. "Going somewhere, girl?"

When I don't answer, Cub clears his throat. "We know what you did, Sir," he says low to Lyon.

I glare sidelong at Lyon then. He turns to Cub. The toothpick goes still.

Cub looks at his feet and blinks fast. "I'm talking about putting Dead End to sleep." His voice breaks apart.

"He was her dog," I squeeze out, my voice thin.

Lyon's big hands come to my shoulders. I don't fight him this time, so he turns me to him. "Dill, didn't you listen to my messages?"

I can't even begin to answer him.

He sighs. "I didn't know you saw the dog that way." Lyon hesitates. "I, uh, didn't even realize, didn't truly understand until talking with G.D. this morning, how furious you've been with me for taking your mother to the hospital. I should have known, but you wouldn't talk and I guess I . . ." He stops, takes in a deep breath as if for strength. "I'm sorry, Dill. Not for the treatments or for taking her to the hospital. I'm sorry because they didn't save her."

His voice trails off. The sadness in it feels like my own, stabs my heart like the sharp point of an ice pick, chips away at the anger with his name on it.

"I thought about what you said—about taking Dead End to Sarah Doyle. The more I thought this over, the more it seemed like a good solution. So I took him to Doc Kitt to get that shoulder wound stitched up and to talk to him about dogs that start running in packs, start killing."

Stunned and unable to speak, my swollen throat convulsing in after-crying hiccups, I stare at Lyon through soggy eyes.

"Kitt explained what's been going on, explained how once dogs start killing, it's near impossible to control or stop them," G.D. puts in. "Instinct takes over."

"That's why I took the dog north to Fairfax County. To Sarah Doyle. She and Mike have always loved Dead

End. And their boys have been itching for a new dog since their old hound died," Lyon adds. "They've got the perfect home for our dog. And they don't have sheep and livestock in their backyard."

"Home?" What is he saying? Even though my tears have slowed, a cloud settles in my head, making me foggy.

"I didn't bring our dog to the Doyle's for retraining, Dill." Lyon's face hardens as he stares into my eyes. "I gave them Dead End. To keep."

An invisible fist plows into my belly, making me suddenly certain that I'm going to throw up. Everything goes blurry from the hot anger that bubbles up inside me. I want to scream, lash out, swing at something, anything. "WHAT?! You did WHAT?!"

Cub sniffs, looks up into Lyon's face. "Dead End hasn't been put to sleep?"

"No," Lyon says without smiling. He glances at me, his eyes alert and maybe even a little afraid. "He'll be kept inside, be confined by a fenced yard, and be taken on lots of long walks, Dill. He won't have much of a chance to run off, but he'll have a fine life."

"That beats any kind of shelter by a long mile, Dill," G.D. tries to tell me.

Cub glances at me, then back at Lyon. "They got groundhogs up by the Doyles?"

I glare at Cub, ready to call him a traitor.

Lyon crinkles his eyebrows at us, looking confused for a second before he focuses back on me. "Giving Dead End to the Doyles is the only way to save his life. It isn't right that we keep a dog that kills sheep. This isn't fair to our neighbors or to their animals. I'm sorry, kiddo, but I really had no other choice."

I'm sorry, kiddo—the words Lyon used to say whenever I got sad, words that always made me feel better. They soothe some, but it's what else he's said that begins to sink into me, calming my belly like peppermint-flavored medicine: He's saved Dead End's life by giving him to the Doyles. This was the best Lyon could do, given his choices. And maybe this is something like what happened with Mom. Maybe he made the best decision he could when it came to taking her to the hospital, too. The thought warms me, spreads slow, and feels like the beginning of something bigger. But most of all, it pulls me a littler closer to him, closer than I've been in months.

Cub steps toward Lyon. "Do the farmers know what you've done, Sir? What about the sheriff and Ms. Hunter?" He shakes his head. "I'm bettin' Ms. Hunter will never let me and Dill near her stable again. And Sheriff Hawks will probably lock us up the minute he sees us."

Good-bye to Cub's career in law enforcement. Good-bye to my riding lessons and the horse shows.

"I don't see you doing jail time," Lyon says in his old, calming tone, as if he is reading my emotions, something he hasn't done in months.

G.D. shakes his head to confirm *no way*.

"Bob Kryer and the farmers mostly want the dog gone," Lyon continues. "And they calmed some when I told them Dill and I would pay them to replace their lost animals, including Fred Barley's steer."

For a second, my stomach clenches again as I picture all my savings going to drippy Mr. Kryer and the farmers. Good-bye to my dream of having my own horse. Good-bye to my stable money.

Lyon closes his eyes, rubs them. "I spoke to the sheriff and Ms. Hunter, told them of my plans before I did anything with Dead End." Lyon chews on the toothpick for a moment. "Sheriff Hawks is spitting mad about the killings, but he's a dog lover."

"Knew I liked that man," G.D. mutters.

"And you know Tucker Hunter has a huge heart," Lyon says, opening his eyes and looking right at me. "In the end, everyone agreed to try my idea of putting Dead End in a home somewhere far away from sheep and farms, rather than having him put to sleep."

Still wet and sniffling, more zombie than girl, my

anger cools to smoldering as I think about Dead End leaving to go searching for Mom, but finding a pack instead. Does this make him a bad dog? Or only a sad dog?

"I gave everyone my word that Dead End would not set a paw within ten miles of this county ever again—and I meant it," Lyon continues, looking hard at me. "But Dill, that's not the end of this mess. You've got to talk with Sheriff Hawks. You'll have some community service to do to atone for your part in this disaster. And Ms. Hunter wants to talk to you, too. She's hurt that you weren't honest with her."

I squirm, as uncomfortable as a horse in a bur blanket.

Lyon's stare drills into me. "But I doubt that either of you will be out of work. And I think Tucker Hunter still wants you to ride her horses, Dill. Even in that regional show coming up. But you've got explaining to do first."

Mucking out a thousand stalls with a teaspoon would be better than facing Sheriff Hawks and Ms. Hunter head-on, but it's clear that no one is giving me a choice in this. I suck in a deep, shaky breath. "Will the farmers . . . ?" I swallow hard. "Will they stop going to your store?"

Lyon pushes his hand back through his hair. The toothpick shifts on his lips. Again, he looks smack into my eyes. "I don't know, Dill. If the killings stop, they might not hold this mess against me."

I focus on my feet. "I'm sorry," I squeak. *For more than you know,* I don't add.

Lyon moves closer to me, and places his hands on my shoulders. "Dill, we'll get through this." He blinks. "We've still got each other." But then he raises his eyebrows, gives the backpack a once-over. "Unless you're leaving."

"To go off wanderin'," G.D. says in a soft, low tone. He stares at the table, shaking his head in his disapproving way.

And then Cub grunts his own disapproval.

Unable to speak from all the feelings wading in my throat, I shake my head *no*.

"Good." Lyon's grip tightens on my shoulders. "Then tomorrow we'll start putting things right. We'll start by going to Fairfax to visit Dead End, maybe even take him with us to visit your mother's grave."

Even though this plan turns me rigid at first, I nod because knowing I'll see that dog again relaxes me some. The time has come for me and Dead End to deal with everything wrapped around Mom being gone. The hurt let out of the smashed jar didn't suffocate me after all. In fact, the crying made me feel lighter, but also stronger somehow. Sure, the pain might still stomp me like an oversized boot, but it won't kill me. I know that now.

Cub jabs his elbow in my side as if trying to knock a

reaction out of me. "Everything will be great after all, Dill."

Possibly. Because Dead End can no longer run off to search for Mom. Because they are together again, in Fairfax. In that way, Lyon has helped our dog to find her. And in a way that I'm not sure I totally understand, Dead End has helped *me* to find her. So now, even though losing Dead End and Mom rips my heart in two places, visiting them both, with Lyon and maybe even G.D. and Cub, feels like the thread that could mend the tears. Once that happens, perhaps I can face life head-on after all.

"There's one more thing." Lyon glances at G.D. and winks.

G.D. smiles. Then Lyon turns and stomps back across the kitchen, through the family room. He opens the door to the garage and disappears.

Cub turns his questioning self to G.D., who, still smiling, focuses on his old hands, folded on the table. Cub raises his eyebrows at me. "What now?"

Wiping at my eyes again, I barely get out a shrug when the garage door opens and closes again and Lyon steps back into the family room.

Cub turns to him. "Jeez!"

I gasp. "Lyon! It's a, a . . ."

"A puppy." A slow, tired smile shifts across my father's face as he offers me the squirming and grunting ball of black fluff.

"A puppy," Cub repeats in a breathy voice that sounds both stunned and amazed at the same time.

"Straight from St. Bernard's Animal Shelter," Lyon adds, his smile becoming real for the first time in a long while. I can almost picture him reaching for his guitar, clearing his throat the way he does before he busts out into a song.

"He's . . . He's . . ." I can't get the words out.

"Cute!" Cub announces, laughing.

"He's a fresh start," Lyon points out.

G.D. bobs his head in agreement.

Cub grins all over. "You saved a puppy, Sir!"

Lyon strokes the wriggling, tiny dog. "If you raise the little guy right, Dill, we'll have a pet that won't take off or threaten other animals."

Even though Lyon holds the puppy out to me, I only stare at the squirming, grunting lump of fluff.

Cub moves to my side, nudges me. So I take the pup, and pull him to my chest. He smells something like warm milk. When he gives me a small grunt and a whimper and licks my chin, my heart goes softer than ice cream in July heat.

Cub strokes the pup's face with one finger. "Guess

you couldn't leave now even if you wanted to, Dill. I mean, you got to stick around and raise this pup. Right?"

I can't help but crack a half smile at the hope in his tone. What would I do without old Cub by my side, talking sense and helping me face things head-on? And for that matter, could I really be happy without Lyon and G.D. around me day by day? I can almost hear Mom whispering in my ear, *Of course not. Now more than ever, you need them as much as they need you.*

So I give the pup a pet, tipping my face down to kiss his forehead. And then I let G.D.'s knapsack slip off my shoulder. It hits the floor with a thud. "Yeah," I say, looking up to meet my father's smile. I guess I will stick around.

ACKNOWLEDGMENTS

First and foremost, I wish to acknowledge, with heartfelt thanks, my agent, Steven Chudney, of the Chudney Agency. I am deeply grateful for his support and guidance, but most of all, for his believing in this novel.

I am also most grateful for my editor, Liz Szabla, who asked all the right questions and offered incredible insights and enthusiasm. I feel so fortunate to have worked with such talent.

Additional gratitude, given with lots of love, goes to the following wonderful people: to my husband, Bill, and my step-daughters, Jessica and Alex. Their patience and support as I worked on the final stages of this novel made it possible. And to my mother, Judy Chapman, my sister, Carey Kopf, and her husband, Rich, for their faith in this dream. And special thanks to Emily, Andrew, and Derek for their inspiration.

Many thanks, too, to my writing group companions and friends, Barbara Ford, Joan Williams, Don Hinkle, Diana Simon, and Kathy Wilford. Their valuable perspectives helped shape this story.

And last but nowhere near least, a big *thank you* to Esta Schwartz and her crew at the Bridgewater, N.J., Barnes and Noble Café for always making a writer feel welcome.